The Other Romanian

The Other Romanian

ANNE ARGULA

A Caravel Mystery
from Pleasure Boat Studio
New York

The Other Romanian
by Anne Argula

ISBN 978-1-929355-85-3
Library of Congress Control Number: 2012932183

Design by Susan Ramundo
Cover by Laura Tolkow
Copy editing by Martin Smith

Pleasure Boat Studio is a proud subscriber to the Green Press Initiative. This program encourages the use of 100% post-consumer recycled paper with environmentally friendly inks for all printing projects in an effort to reduce the book industry's economic and social impact. With the cooperation of our printing company, we are pleased to offer this book as a Green Press book.

Pleasure Boat Studio books are available through the following:
SPD (Small Press Distribution) Tel. 800-869-7553, Fax 510-524-0852
Partners/West Tel. 425-227-8486, Fax 425-204-2448
Baker & Taylor Tel. 800-775-1100, Fax 800-775-7480
Ingram Tel. 615-793-5000, Fax 615-287-5429
Amazon.com and **bn.com**

and through
PLEASURE BOAT STUDIO: A LITERARY PRESS
www.pleasureboatstudio.com
201 West 89th Street
New York, NY 10024

Contact **Jack Estes**
Fax: 888-810-5308
Email: pleasboat@nyc.rr.com

TO MY CREW:

The Tobster, Li'l Sheba, and El Gizmo

Man arrested after trying to sell bookmark tied to Hitler

Sting recovers item stolen in 2002

An 18-karat bookmark that Adolf Hitler's mistress reportedly gave him 65 years ago for solace after Germany lost an epic battle ended up this week in a Starbucks parking lot, allegedly peddled by a Romanian businessman.

News item: Seattle *Post-Intelligencer,* November 27, 2008

One

Who has my cell phone number?

I mean, who *else* has my cell phone number, not counting the dead man lying in the chilly drizzle down on the waterfront? Does my pill-pushing ex-husband have it? No, nor his new love Esther, the punchboard emeritus of Lewis and Clark High School, now queen of the Spokane Rite-Aid. Friends have I few and those few don't have it. My son Nelson has it and once in a blue moon will call me when his amphibious squadron goes ashore at Little Creek, Virginia. Two or three unreliable sources have it programmed into their own phones, and of course it is always close at hand to Sergeant Beckman, pride of the Seattle PD.

I mean, even I don't have the number. If you asked me to write it down, I couldn't. So who *did* write it down and how did it get into a dead man's pocket?

I happen to have a pathological relationship to the telephone. This won't help.

It was one of those Northwest mornings, one of more than there used to be, when you question everything about yourself, from the pulsing of that vein in the crook of your arm to why you are living the way you do, and when I say you I mean me. I never took a vow. Yes, I did take an oath as a spanking new cop in LA, and I kept it through my last watch in Spokane; but truth, justice, and the American way, though I love them all dearly, don't have to be on me anymore. There are younger people for that. I've got a trick knee, an entry-and-exit wound just below the bottom rib, between the liver and the large intestine, and a susceptibility for hot flashes that would bring Vampira to her knees. In short, I don't need it anymore, though at the moment—that is, the moment before my cell phone rang—I might not have been dwelling on all that. Doesn't matter. I'd already crunched the numbers. When Connors and I split, since we made about the same money, I walked away with half the pot, including a half-interest in a house that had appreciated crazy much. I took early retirement from the SPD and my dignity. I could do whatever I wanted to do. There were scads of things out there to do that didn't involve finding and fingering folks. I'd given this subject some thought. Of all the things I might do, there is only one that I know I can't do: nothing. It's a pity, because if less is more, nothing must be everything. I offer this rare bit of introspection hoping that as the story unfolds, a parallel will be noticed. Maybe not.

When my phone went off that morning of my discontent, I flipped my latte grande and shuffled a St. Vitus dance on the puddle, right in the middle of Starbucks—the one in my building—and then I leapt into one of my signature hot flashes. My toes were on fire, my hair crackled, sending wisps of smoke ceilingward. As the prints were peeling off my fingertips, flames shot out of my flared nostrils. (All this is metaphorical. I hope.)

Cash, the boy barista who unaccountably treats me like his mother, rushed from his station and led me to a table. "Relax, Quinn, I'll get you another one." He waved for someone to mop up the mess I'd made. I tried to smile, but the Motorola kept sniping at me. "Should I answer that for you?" asked Cash. I nodded.

He gingerly reached into the breast pocket of my North Face vest and opened the phone. "Hello?"

I could hear the gruff voice on the other end. "Who's this?"

"Who are you calling?" said Cash, nobody's dummy.

"You tell me," said the voice, with a bit of authority.

"Hey, you're the one who called," said Cash.

"Seattle Police Department. Now you."

"Hold on." He handed the phone to me. "*La Placa*," he said, which is Spanish for the cops.

I took the phone. My burners had backed down.

"This is Quinn."

"Jesus, I should have known it would be you."

Now I recognized the voice.

"What do you want, Beckman? And why wouldn't it be me?"

"I should have known this would turn out to be your number."

"Huh? You called it, didn't you?"

"I'm down on Alaskan Way, south of Main, standing over a dead body."

"Well, that can't be good."

A cadaver on Alaskan Way, though unfortunate and probably still a little newsworthy, was not exactly earth shaking. Hit by SUVs rushing on or off a ferry, or poisoned by alcohol, or fished out of the Sound—thrown there by themselves as often as otherwise—dead guys on Alaskan Way are not entirely unprecedented.

"Anybody I know?" I asked out of politeness.

"That's why I'm calling."

"What's why?"

"Because this dude has got no ID. Nada."

"And this involves me how?"

"It involves you like this: upon inventorying the body on the scene, all we find is a matchbook with your phone number written on the inside. Which is why I dialed it. Imagine my surprise."

"Cause of death? Just curious."

"Beaten severely about the head and shoulders, finished off with a coup de grace to the back of the head, calibre not yet known."

"Da frick."

Whatever happened, it happened within walking distance of where I'd done my "So You Think You Can Dance" audition. I was a little surprised that I hadn't heard the sirens from my apartment. As of late, however, the ringing in my ears was hitting hard at high-C, which is why I keep the volume up on NPR while I'm getting dressed for the day. And living downtown anywhere in America you just get used to hearing sirens, like out on the flats you learn to sleep through the midnight express even though you can spit on the tracks from your crib and you've given up all hope of hopping on. Or under. I carried my replacement latte down Yesler, ducking my babushka into the cold wet wind.

This was in early November, our onset of despair up here on the left-hand corner of the map, the start of the long, gray, wet, and often cold winter. In November come the winds from the north, shivering, maddening winds. It's even money out on the islands that your power will go off on Thanksgiving Day, so everyone has a Weber fired up and ready. That way you can quickly carry the roasting turkey from a dead oven to the hot barbecue. We grit our teeth and hold on until January, when we can delude ourselves into believing that we're halfway through the worst of it.

Because of the crime scene, the waterfront was jammed with traffic. I threw the dangling end of my scarf over my shoulder, held onto the strap of my purse, and hurried toward the ado.

Beckman was standing a few feet from the body, his hands in the pockets of a navy-blue wool Façonnable jacket. Give the flatfoot his due, he had a sense of fashion. He made regular forays through Nordstrom Rack, snagging only the primo stuff: Façonnable, Hugo Boss, and size twelve-and-a-half Cole and Hahns.

The victim lay face down, to the south, hands near his sides, an oversized gray hoodie covering most of his head. He had on a pair of brown corduroys, well worn and ragged at the cuffs.

Someone from the department was pulling off the hiking boots and looking inside of them. A couple of homicide cops questionned witnesses. A photographer took pictures.

I stopped and stood next to Beckman.

"Cinnamon dolce or anything like that?" he asked, eyeing my drink.

"Nothing sweet around me," I assured him, and handed him the drink.

"Copy that."

"Fuck you."

"Nice mouth."

"Hormone depletion. It makes me impatient."

"Like you weren't already."

"You didn't know me then."

"Wouldn't have wanted to."

"Copy that."

He took a long swallow and handed back the coffee. "Thanks."

We had to raise our voices because of the wind. So we moved under a shelter

I looked over the rail and down at the murky waters of Puget Sound. "Somebody," I said, "could have popped him, tossed the gun over the rail, and got into a car. A minute later, tsk, tsk, look at the drunk on the sidewalk."

Seattle streets used to be littered with drunks and panhandlers, then not so much. Now they seem to be back. Still, a tsk-tsk would have been socially conscious enough until someone noticed the guy wasn't breathing.

"No rings, no watch," said Beckman. "What do you think, five-ten or so?"

"About that."

"Hundred and seventy? Mid-thirties?"

"Close enough. Does kind of look professional," I observed. Which hardly ever happens in our town, where the ethos is to do things for yourself.

"It is what it is." He took a pause and said, "I still don't understand what that means.' The thing is what it is.' What else could it be?"

"Comes to murder, it never is what it is. It's always something else."

"Don't mess with me."

"I'm here. I guess I ought to have a look," I said.

"Be my guest." He talked to the shoe guy. "Frances, let Quinn have a look at him."

I stepped around the body and squatted with Frances, who pulled back the hood and turned the lifeless face toward me. It was black and blue and puffy. Someone had worked him over immodestly. It was hard to say what he used to look like. He had brown thinning hair and a charred hole where it tapered down his neck.

"I don't know him from Adam," I told Beckman.

I straightened up, and since we'd had a proper introduction, I stepped over the dead man and stood again next to Beckman.

"The beating don't look fresh," he said, "but the bullet hole does."

"Beat him up, bring him here a couple days later, and shoot him on the street. Doesn't make a lot of sense."

"No. Could be the guys who beat him up might not be the guys who shot him."

"In other words, you got nothing."

"I got him," he said, nodding at the stiff.

"Me, I'd send a diver down. Water can't be too deep."

"Might be he'll find another body or two."

I chuckled. You can't help it sometimes.

"You thinking drugs?" I asked.

"I'm always thinking drugs. Would that account for your number?"

"You know me better than that."

"Yeah, you're a juicer."

"Hardly even that, but I'm willing to try."

"Drugs unleash a certain fury. Irrational violence. Not the use of them, just the sale of them."

"Say he was shot somewhere else and dumped here."

"Why here? Too many witnesses."

"How many do you have?"

The answer was none.

"You don't shoot a guy on Alaskan Way and then empty out his pockets."

"The reverse is true. You sure you never saw him before? You meet a lot of people."

"As few as I can," I said.

Beckman had that distant stare. Across the street and under the viaduct, a blind man was walking with a seeing-eye yellow Labrador. We both watched him for a moment. Beckman wondered aloud, "When a seeing-eye dog takes a dump, how does the blind man scoop the poop?"

"How's he even know the dog's taking a poop?"

"Oh, he can tell. His other senses are way keen."

"Wish ours were."

"He gets a pass, I guess. Handicapped."

"Anyway, the stuff's organic."

"Lot of organic stuff, you still wouldn't want it on the street. Like this dude for example. He's organic. Wish I knew why he had your number."

"Me too. Whoever cleaned and clocked him missed it or didn't care."

"I mean, why *your* number?"

"Let me see it."

"What?"

"The number, where it's written down."

He handed me a small plastic envelope. A matchbook was inside, in the open position. None of the matches had been used. Written with a thick pencil, there it was: my cell phone number.

"Whoa. You didn't tell me about this."

"What?"

"The seven. It's a European seven, with the slash across."

"Oh, yeah."

"So this guy could be European, if he wrote the number."

"Or an arty American."

"Or anything else, if he wasn't the one who wrote it."

"Or it could be a miswrite."

"Yeah, but the seven is still a seven."

"Miswrites happen all the time. Somebody gives somebody their number and the guy gets it wrong. Calls the other guy and it's a wrong number."

"So why carry it? You throw it away."

"Anybody call recently?"

"Yeah, you, and I freaked out then. You know how I am with cell phones."

"Hey, a cell phone saved your life once."

"Which might account for some of why they freak me out."

That was a time when we both screwed up. You can read about it. I don't talk about it anymore. I thought Beckman didn't either. I looked at him like I thought we didn't talk about that anymore?

"Sorry," he said, and then changed the subject. "How's the apartment going"

"I don't really know."

I'd recently been informed that my landlord wanted to sell the condo I was living in. He wanted my cooperation in showing the place to prospective buyers, like there were any now that the bubble had burst. I reminded him that I had four months left on my lease and it didn't say anything about my obligation to let strangers come poking around the premises when I don't even allow friends up there. He said maybe I should buy it myself since I was already so settled. I said maybe I should, if he made it real easy for me, since suddenly it was a buyer's market, if a buyer could get a loan, which this one might not be able to, recently divorced and all that. These conversations were conducted through an agent. I'd never met my landlord.

"You gonna buy it?"

"Seriously considering it."

"Time might be right. Prices going down. Sure you don't know this guy?"

"How many times do I have to tell you?" I was still looking at the matchbook in the plastic bag. "He wasn't a smoker."

"'Could have been. He just didn't use any of these matches. Autopsy'll tell us that."

"Okay, he grabs the matchbook and writes down the number. Or someone, a European, does and gives it to him. My number, it turns out. We don't know why."

"Might be we know where." He turned over the bag and showed me the other side. The Copper Gate. "Ever been there?"

"Never even heard of it."

"It's over in Ballard."

"Then I wouldn't have." Ballard was a neighborhood of old Scandanavians, the land of the slow-moving Volvos and endless turn signals. I flipped the bag over and looked at the number again. The writing on the matchbook was thick. "This wasn't written with an ordinary pencil," I said. "Ordinary pencils don't go bigger than point-o-nine mil. This looks like maybe it was written with one of those lead holders, like artists sketch with. Could be John Doe was an artist."

"He doesn't look like an artist."

"What's missing?"

"A beard? An artistic flair? Look at how he's dressed. Maybe he was a carpenter, with a carpenter's pencil. More likely."

"Or it could be he didn't write it, or somebody borrowed somebody's pencil to write it."

"Could be."

"So in other words, you've got nothing."

"I still got him."

"Okay, maybe he's at The Copper Gate—everybody's got to be somewhere—and there's an artist there sketching."

"Or a carpenter."

"Doing what?"

"Carpenter work."

"Can I have the artist?"

"Sure."

"Thank you."

"You know why it's called The Copper Gate?" he asked.

"Pray tell."

"You'll like this. It was one of Seattle's original dives, owned and operated by a woman of a certain age and brassiness, who for an hour or so before closing time would take off all her clothes and serve drinks naked."

"Why?"

"'Cause she could."

"Yeah? So?"

"She was a redhead." Beckman smiled. "The copper gate."

I might have sighed, the way you do around men who tell stories about naked women.

"Okay," said Beckman. "You got the artist sketching. Sketching what?"

"This famous dive with the colorful past."

"That happens. Like in Paris, or the movies."

"You've been to Paris?"

"No, I've been to the movies."

"Well, it happens in real life, too. I've seen it."

"Where?"

"At the Market, for example."

"Okay."

"This yonko and the artist strike up a conversation."

"Why?"

"Some people like to meet strangers and be social."

"Maybe the artist is a good-looking woman."

"Which is the only reason dogs like you talk to anybody, when you're not drunk."

"Even then."

"They're having a conversation. This guy asks the artist if he . . . or she . . . knows of an excellent private investigator in town, because he's a stranger here and he has some shit hanging over him. The artist grabs a matchbook and writes down my number on it."

"How's the artist have your number?"

"I don't know."

"You have any artist clients?"

"They can't afford me."

"Explain me this. The artist has her sketchbook, why didn't she use a page from that?"

"Why waste a page when she could just grab a matchbook?"

"Could have used a little corner only."

"That still would have ruined the whole page."

"Somebody has your number and a thick pencil. Why? Gives it to John Doe. Why? It's all the dude has on him when he punches out on cold wet Alaskan Way on a miserable morning. Why? We must ascertain all that."

"*We*? Ascertain *this*," I said.

"Aren't you curious? It's a mystery."

"Show me a cop who likes a mystery and I'll show you a yonko in the wrong line of work."

He didn't contradict me.

"My feeling? This fellow isn't from around here," I said.

"What makes you think so?"

"His boots look funny."

"So do yours."

"And anybody writing down a local number for a local guy wouldn't write down the one and two-o-six area code. They'd just write down the number. And why the *one* anyway? Everybody knows you have to dial *one*. Unless this guy is from another country."

"Ah, so now we do have something."

"We again? I don't think so. There's no *we* here. There's only you and this guy."

Two

I crossed First Avenue intending to get another coffee before clocking in at my office, which is just across the street in the Pioneer Building, but I saw Sammi Lou hovering just outside the entrance to the condos where I live. She intercepted me on the corner before I could make it into Starbucks.

"Morning, Quinn," she called out.

Sammi Lou—her father must have wanted a boy—was about my age and facing up to some deferred maintenance. A lifetime of high heels had recently necessitated some surgery and she was hobbling around with one of those ugly black velcro boots on her right foot, the thick white sock below it collecting dirty rainwater.

"Should you be getting that wet?" I asked.

"No! But I have to make a living." The heady days for real estate agents were over, and hard times were spurring everyone to work even harder and keep themselves a moving target. "I was hoping I'd bump into you."

"Looks like you were lying in wait."

"I am not stalking you, but I do have a nice couple from Austin, Texas, very interested in your unit, if I could just show it to them. It would not be an inconvenience."

"Well, it would be. I've explained that."

"I understand, but the owner is super motivated to sell, and, frankly, I don't want to lose these Texans, unless you've given more thought to buying it yourself."

In the special language of real estate agents, what was she saying? That if I didn't buy the apartment we'd have two more Texans in Seattle? Since when is that my responsibility? I told her I had, in fact, given it more thought.

"Can I buy you a latte?" she offered.

We went inside and stood in line. When she reached into her lumpy shoulder bag to pay, the head of a tiny silky terrier poked out. The dog was content to stay in his bag and watch us as we sat and talked.

"Thing is," I said, "six-fifty is way high for one bedroom and a bath."

"Not for this building. Not really. It's small, private, great view . . ."

She ran out of amenities.

"The bubble has burst, Sammi Lou."

"That's right, and you probably won't see the wild appreciation we have been enjoying, but downtown condos are still hot. It's a good investment for the future, Quinn."

"Only I'm not investing, and I got a great future behind me. All I'm doing is trying not to have to move again."

"I know. It sucks to move. Make an offer. Who knows?"

We talked for another few minutes, but I stayed on the fence. The idea of going six hundred and fifty thousand into debt, if I could even find a bank to lubricate that, for the joy of living in a one-bedroom, one-bath apartment with a view of Pioneer Square and a slice of Puget Sound was hard for me to get my graying head around. My parents paid nine thousand for their house. Even now, for what I would have to pay for a small apartment in Seattle I could get a horse ranch in Kentucky, including the nags. Problem is, I don't want to live in Kentucky and I don't trust horses, not much more than I trust real estate agents.

Still, once back in my office, I penciled and papered the numbers and listed the pros and cons of home ownership. It was hard to concentrate. I kept going back to the dead man on Alaskan Way. I couldn't stop thinking that, somehow, it was my number that led to that man's murder. If I'd had a case of my own I wouldn't have to be thinking about Beckman's John Doe.

I called my favorite cop. He was still at the crime scene.

"Any witnesses yet?" I asked.

"Not so far."

"Listen, what if someone planted my number on him *after* he was dead?"

"Why would someone do that?"

"Because why else would it be there? Somebody took his wallet, his phone, his keys, . . . why not the matchbook?"

"They missed it or didn't want it, like you said."

"I said that?"

"Who'd plant your number on a John Doe?"

"I don't know."

"We checked out the boots."

"Unusual boots."

"Quality stuff. AKU Suiterra hiking boots, made in Romania."

"That might account for the European seven, *if* John Doe's a Romanian *and* he wrote the number himself."

"Like someone told him the number and he wrote it down?"

"Like that."

"Still doesn't mean he's European. His boots were made there but most American shoes are made somewhere else. Most everything is made somewhere else."

"So you still got nothing."

"More than I did. I'll keep you in the loop."

"I don't want to be in the loop. Only one more thing, where did you find the matchbook, in his pants or his hoodie?"

"Hoodie. In the pouch. Why?"

"Well, somebody might borrow somebody's hoodie, but you wouldn't borrow their pants."

"I wouldn't."

"Neither would I."

"So maybe this guy has nothing to do with your number; it's the guy whose hoodie it is, whose hoodie he maybe borrowed."

"Just another possible."

"I'm smiling a little right now."

"Why's that?"

"You're on the case."

One thing leads to another in life, which isn't always a lot of fun, especially when it leads to a dead man on a cold, wet street. I didn't like being a part of it, no matter how remote.

When I want to take my mind off something unpleasant I think about where I might have lunch. Salumi's? Bakeman's? Splurge at the Metropolitan?

While I was trying to decide, the phone rang and made the decision for me. This time, in the safety of my office, I answered it like a normal person.

"This is Quinn."

"Hello, Quinn, this is Shelley Lavendar. We've never met but I think you know who I am?"

"Give me a hint."

"Shelley Lavendar Krapp. I've gone back to my maiden name."

"Can't say I blame you."

Nearly two years earlier, her husband, Alex Krapp, was a client. He was an A-list screenwriter who hired me to verify the existence of a fifteen-year-old boy he had emotionally adopted as his son. Over the phone. Krapp was like a father to the boy, despite never having seen him in the flesh because the boy was too sick to have visitors. In fact, he was terminally sick. Alex Krapp had most of himself invested in that relationship. Me, I just did my job. It wasn't that hard, really, though shots were fired. The hardest part was the unsettling pull Alex Krapp had on me, in what was then my 'vulnerable state,' commonly called. At the time, he wasn't on solid ground himself, though not because of me. His wife was living apart from him, in Santa Barbara, while he worked with actors who collected twenty million dollars for a hundred bucks worth of aping, and with directors who after a youth of satisfying themselves were now in their middle years banging fashion models two at a time. Then into his life came this kid, a whole new reality, the best of humanity, the most fulfilling connection he had in the world. Krapp was pretty much undone by the process of my finding Danny. Right after that he took it on the arfy-darfy from Seattle, straddling his Harley-Davidson Road King. He was never seen nor heard from again. The conventional wisdom had it that the aging screenwriter went over the edge of Route 1, somewhere around Big Sur, disappearing into the Pacific. Back then, when I was on the clock, he had talked to me only briefly about his wife. (I asked.) He might have mentioned a few things about her, but I don't recall that he ever actually told me her name. He had no reason to. I wasn't interested in her name or much else about her, apart from how she could let a good man like that get away, but then I've let one or two get away myself, and I wouldn't like to have to explain it either.

"And I feel," said the voice at the other end of the line, "that I know you. Alex talked about you."

Do we ever get out of high school? He *talked* about me! I flushed. "What did he say?"

"He said you worked out of Seattle and you were very good at what you do. Maybe *too* good."

The flush kept coming.

"Where are you calling from?" I asked.

"Here. I'm in Seattle. Hopefully not for long. This rain, this wind . . ."

"It's not the rain, it's the gray."

I remembered Krapp told me that the Northwest weather tarnished his wife's sheen and she detested LA. While her husband divided his time between Hollywood and Bainbridge Island, at least during that last year, she lived with two Irish wolfhounds in sunny Montecito, the even nicer part of Santa Barbara. She and Alex stayed married but neither of them seemed to know why. That's as much as I remembered, or cared to.

Of course, I wondered why she was calling me, but sometimes nothing is the best of all things to say.

"I understand people who move up here don't care about the rain," she said. "They just have to be here."

"Yeah, I wish I knew why."

She wasn't talking about people, she was talking about her late husband, and she wanted me to talk about him, too.

"Can you explain his need for a cold, wet island?" she asked me.

"Me? That's something a wife might be able to explain."

"But you got to know each other quite well, didn't you?"

"Not that well."

"Better than you admit, I think."

"If this is some kind of delayed confrontation, I've got nothing to confess."

Everybody says that, but everybody really does have something to confess. Anyway, it's not about what you *felt*, it's about what you *did*, and I didn't do anything. My regret.

"I really don't care," she said. "I know a connection was made, but it doesn't matter."

Again with the flush, the kind you get when you're sixteen, not the crappy kind you get when you're fifty.

"You're probably wondering why I'm here?"

She raised her tone at the end, making it a question.

"No, people come and go. I'm wondering why you called me."

"I think Alex might still be alive."

"Oh?"

"If he's not, he might have been a victim of someone." Maybe of you, I thought, but I stifled. "Could we meet? I'm downtown, shopping. I was going to have my hair done, but with this rain, like, why bother?"

Me, I don't even own a hairbrush. I shake my fingers through my hair and call it done. Every so often I get it cut at the Bocz Salon. Lately I've been stewing about whether or not I should start coloring or give it up to the inevitable.

"You still there?"

"Still here."

"Are you free for lunch?"

"I may be available but I'm never free."

"Where can we meet?"

Three

SCANDANAVIAN SINCE 1946.

I passed the place and had to make a U-turn. I parked a block away and walked back. Its frontage had nothing to commend it. It looked like any other low-rent Seattle tavern.

Inside The Copper Gate, two themes tried to complement each other: Norse shipping and naked women. Clear transparencies hung above the beverage case along with original black-velvet art reminiscent of Tijuana pre-drug wars. Two enormous breasts hung above the aquavit chiller, and scores of suggestive snapshots festooned the walls. An exit to God-knows-where was fashioned to look like a giant vagina, complete with a clitoris. The bar itself was rigged to look like the prow of an old Viking ship, the galley aft. Half a dozen barstools faced the starboard side, the port side blending into a bulkhead, behind which flickered an antique black-and-white floor-model television set. Back from the barstools was another long, curving, free-standing bulkhead, separating a section . . . for what? Lovers? Leaning against the opposing wall was an almost life-size painting—nude of course—of Nada, the founding redhead. The sail of the ship was made entirely of nude pictures, some bordering on the lewd. Only two of the eight tables were occupied, by what seemed to be what was left of the grunge movement, slurping fish-cake soup and dreaming of poetic justice and a brand-new sound.

I sat at the bar. The bartender, a fair-haired boy named Lars, possibly hired for his ethnicity, gave me a pleasant hello and asked what I'd like to have. Over his head hung a huge stuffed and mounted king salmon.

"I'm meeting somebody for lunch," I said. "I'll just wait."

"Let me know if you want anything."

"Could I have a book of matches, please?"

"Oh, there's no smoking anymore in Seattle."

"For later."

He took a book out of the bowl behind the bar and slid it toward me. It matched the one Beckman found on the dead body that morning.

I slipped the matches into my parka jacket and looked up at the fish. I could almost make out the inscription on the brass plate. I stood up and leaned closer, standing on tiptoes to read it. I could not believe what I was reading:

> King Salmon, 61½ pounds,
> landed by Alex Krapp,
> Langerra Island, B.C.

The law of dives narrows down the six degrees of separation to about half. I may not know you, for instance, but we've been to the same dive. Still, the coincidence was freaky. It wasn't that hard to believe Alex Krapp was a fisherman, but I had a difficult time picturing the Hollywood screenwriter, a regular at The Ivy, adding to the eccentric décor of The Copper Gate.

"That's some fish," I said.

"Yeah, the guy who caught it used to come in here. He had this fish that he didn't know what to do with, so the boss told him if he hung it here he would comp him for life."

"What a deal."

"It would have been, only the guy didn't live much longer."

"Really? Lost at sea?"

"No, on the road. He was a screenwriter."

"He must have been a regular."

"Not really, but he came in when he was in town. He spent most of his time down in LA."

"So this screenwriter, when he did come in, did he come in alone or did he bring anybody?"

Lars knew it was now beyond small talk over a bar. "Why do you want to know?" I gave him my card. "Hey, wow, you're a detective?"

"Surprised?"

"Yeah, I thought you were just a . . ."

"A what?"

"Just a lady."

I knew he was going to say 'another old lady.' He saved himself a little abuse.

"Are you working on a case?"

"Not yet."

"The screenwriter? His disappearance and all?"

"Well, it is a mystery."

You think somebody else was involved?"

"Somebody else is always involved."

"I do remember him coming in with another guy. Or maybe they just wound up here together at times, but they used to have some serious talks, head to head."

"What guy?"

"He called him Bogdan. He had an accent."

"How do you spell that?"

"Dunno."

"Was that his first name or his last name?"

"Don't know that either. I'm not even sure it *was* his name."

"You know what kind of accent?"

"Eastern Europe. Russian maybe."

"How old?"

"Mid-thirties?"

"You asking me?"

"Hey, I couldn't tell your age."

"I didn't ask you to. I *know* how old I am. Was he a tall man, short man?"

"Average. Five-nine, ten. Medium build, brown hair. Ordinary-looking guy."

The description fit lots of men. That's why they call it average. Like, it fit Beckman's John Doe.

My phone dinged, just once. It made me jump, of course, but I was okay with it. A text message.

"Excuse me," I said and opened my phone.

Bruno had texted me this message: "Stefano must die! Again!"

Four

I re-read the three-word message. The problem was, I didn't know any Stefano. Nor did I know anyone named Bruno. Was Stefano the dead man on Alaskan Way? How many more strangers were in possession of my cell phone number?

A shaft of light fell over my shoulder. I turned and saw Shelley Lavendar come through the door. I knew it had to be her. She was a woman aging very gracefully, from her expensive black boots up a pair of killer legs, to the Burberry trench coat with matching scarf. She was a woman who spent some time and money and attention on herself, the kind of woman I could never be, not even with a two-year subscription to ***Elle***. She wore sunglasses in a town that hadn't seen the sun since Columbus Day, and her long dark hair was covered with a scarf, reminding me a bit of Jackie O, the pictures I've seen of her back in the day. She carried two shopping bags: one from J. Gilbert Shoes and one from Seattle Art. Over her shoulder she was burdened with what looked like a newly purchased Patagonia duffel, full of something lumpy.

She took a quick glance around, making eye contact with me, then slipped behind the curved bulkhead and into the concealed booth.

Before going over to her, I said to Lars, "Listen, kid, the police are going to be talking to you soon." He looked struck. "It has nothing to do with you or what we were talking about here. You and I were just passing time."

"What's going on?" he asked nervously.

"Nothing. It's all about a book of matches."

I left him wondering about that and, my phone still in hand, went to sit down with Shelley Lavendar.

With the raincoat off she looked even better, a drop-dead figure made leaner by the black sweater and tight black leather pants. No doubt she had a personal trainer, or two. She looked up at me.

"Yeah, I'm Quinn," I said and sat opposite her. I didn't take off my parka. It's not that I was ashamed of my own figure, though I have to admit it isn't a point of pride with me, but I wasn't sure how long I'd be staying.

"Thanks for seeing me," she said. She studied me long enough to make both of us uneasy, the way I used to study Esther, my ex's trollop. Her smile was—what?—wan?

"You picked an out-of-the-way place. It's a twenty-dollar cab ride."

"You look like you can afford it."

"I can, but I'm riding back with you."

"How do you know I'm not on a motorcycle?"

"Well, it would give you *something* in common with my husband."

She was no pushover. I took off my parka.

"So, your husband might still be alive?" I put it as a question

Before she could answer, Lars had come out from behind the bar to take our order.

I went for a Danish aquavit, clear, and some *sursild*, which the menu translated as pickled herring, beets, and pumpernickel. I've always had a sweet tooth for the little fish. She ordered the *blomkals soppa*, a spiced cauliflower soup with lemon oil, and a glass of O Chardonnay, a snappy little upstart from the Yakima Valley.

I nodded to the side, over the curving bulkhead and toward the mounted salmon, and said, "Remember that?"

She took off the shades, leaned over, and looked up at the fish for a long moment before saying, "What?"

"The king salmon. I didn't know Alex was a fisherman."

"That's his? I'm glad it found a home. But why here, of all places?"

"Seems he hung out here."

"Alex? You're kidding."

"You didn't know?"

"I never knew where Alex chose to hang out. I didn't know that he even hung out."

"It does seem an odd place for him."

"He was a restless spirit. He used to say he could never find a place to sit."

"Where?"

"Anywhere. In the house, in the world."

"There was that rocking chair," I said.

"Which rocking chair?"

"The one overlooking the bay."

"You were in the house?"

"No, he just told me he liked to sit there."

I'm a literal person, so cite me.

"He couldn't sit there either, not for long. Wherever he was, he didn't feel he belonged. Whatever he had, he didn't feel it could be his, including me." She caught herself starting to wax dramatic and put the brakes on. "Oh, well, why try to figure it all out now. Life's too short."

"Not during a Seattle winter."

"Is Alex the reason you wanted to meet here?"

"Pure coincidence. I didn't even know he had ever been here."

"How strange!"

"He used to come here with a guy."

"A guy?"

"A friend, I guess."

"What was his name?"

"Bogdan."

I watched her eyes for any flash of recognition. Nothing.

"The guy had an accent," I said. Ah, there, a little flicker. "You know him?"

"No, but he had Seattle friends I didn't know. Obviously."

"I thought he was a loner."

"Well . . . even a loner has an acquaintance or two. What kind of accent?"

"Eastern European, according to Lars the bartender. Do you know of any friend he may have had with an Eastern European accent or any other kind of accent?"

"Sure. Movie people. Lots of them have accents. But lots of people everywhere have accents. Maybe this person was a fishing buddy."

"That's probably it. So why did you want to have lunch with me?" I asked her.

"Apart from the fact that you might have fallen in love with my husband and I wanted to have a good look at you?" I didn't answer. I didn't know how. Might have? Fallen? In love? "And I already told you, I think Alex might still be alive."

"Then you're one of a dwindling few."

"Are you still among them?"

"What makes you think I ever was?"

"I read your book. I got an advance copy."

"How? I just got mine."

"Your publisher sent it. I guess because I'm in it." She paused, waiting for me to deny it. Which I didn't. "For a mystery it's a bit enigmatic. I mean, in the way most mysteries aren't."

"I don't write mysteries. I write memoirs in small doses, which is the only way you should have to take one."

"Congratulations on all your success, anyway."

"What success? If they were successful I wouldn't be sticking my nose in other people's business."

"How do you decide which cases to write about?"

"Don't worry, I won't write about you."

"Not any more than you have already?"

"Really?"

"There were a few references. Not very flattering." I wasn't going to be offering any excuses. "Don't worry, I won't sue. I know you were attracted to Alex. I don't think he ever realized it. He was that way. What do you suppose he will think, if he ever reads the book?"

"Well, I'm not even sure he's alive, am I?"

"Look, I don't feel threatened. Okay? Our marriage was stalled. Maybe it was broken completely. I don't know. I always held out some hope, but then so did his other two wives. Naturally, I'm curious about you, but my only purpose here is to find out what happened to Alex."

"Would he have come to see you in Santa Barbara, on that road trip?"

"He said he would. He called me and said he was on his way. Either he didn't make it or he changed his mind or . . . I don't know. I need to find out, once and for all."

"You read my book?"

"Yes, in one sitting. That's how I know you never really believed he crashed his bike into the ocean."

"I kept an open mind."

"And now?"

"I'm on to other things."

"But don't you wonder from time to time?"

I wonder *all* the time. Sometimes it keeps me awake at night. I didn't tell her that. I said, "Once in a while."

"I'll pay whatever you ask."

"Well, those are the right words, but the California Highway Patrol and police in several juristictions have come to a dead end on it, excuse the expression."

"I don't think they care too much about missing adults."

"You're right. People go missing all the time. It's not illegal. They drop out and stay out."

"Do you think Alex did that?"

"Maybe. What makes you think he's still alive?"

"Recently a large package was delivered to my home in Montecito . . ."

Lars arrived with our order, but neither one of us paid much attention. She leaned closer to me.

"It was full of cassettes. Alex's."

"I still have about twenty myself."

"You do?"

I could see this was unexpected news but I couldn't see why it might be something to get excited about.

"Yeah, he gave them to me when I was working on his case, just so I could know the voices of the principals."

"I'd like to have them, please."

I'd thought about throwing them out, many times, but would wind up just moving them around again. They weren't mine, so I didn't have the right to destroy them. Technically, they belonged to his next of kin. This lady, it would seem.

"Sure," I told her. "You can have them. The other cassettes, in your package, where did they come from?"

"I don't know. They were hand delivered."

"Maybe Gwendolyn, his secretary, sent them."

"No, she sent everything when they closed up his office."

"Your husband was a bit obsessive about taping conversations. Was he that obsessive about playing them back?"

"He spent so much time alone, who knows what he did or what he obsessed about? Why do you ask?"

"Well, it's possible he loaded up his saddlebags with cassettes for the trip. You know, to listen to them, sort things out."

"If that's true, the fact that I have them now proves he didn't fly off some cliff into the ocean."

"Unless he sent them to somebody else before he went over the cliff."

"Who? He would have sent them to me. I know he would."

"Unless he didn't want you to hear them."

"Then why do I have them now?"

"Somebody else might want you to hear them. Have you listened to them?"

"Some. He had a cataloging code that's impossible to decipher, but several of the cassettes were definitely made during his trip. I marked them for you."

"For me? What am I supposed to do with them?"

With her booted foot she pushed the duffel bag across the floor to my own feet.

"I want you to listen to them, especially to the ones I marked. They document his trip. I want you to retrace his path and find out what happened to my husband."

Five

We ate our lunch mostly in silence, while Shelley gave me a chance to mull over her proposition. I was happy for the distraction away from Bruno and why he wanted Stefano dead. Again. And why he wanted me to know, via his text message. I didn't want to think that maybe Stefano was already dead, or about how I fit into this unhappy picture, if I did at all, which I hoped I didn't.

If I said yes to Shelley I would once again have a case of my own, which would get me out of Beckman's, which would be a beautiful thing. It would take me out of town as well, which might not be such a bad thing. I didn't want to leave town, but that's an on-going problem. I never want to leave town, not because I'm in love with the place—maybe a little—but because I do not like to travel and everybody knows that about me. I especially do not like road trips, which this certainly would be.

Shelley took a small leather pad from her purse and withdrew from it a miniature silver pen. She wrote down her cell phone number and slid it across the table to me. I glanced at it and saw it had a 206 prefix.

"I thought you lived in Santa Barbara."

"I do."

"You have a two-o-six number."

"Oh, that. When Alex signed up for a cell phone up here, he got one for me too, and put us on the family plan. It's such a wonderful number, I can't give it up."

It was an enviable number. It ended in two doubles.

"You know, you could hire anybody for this," I told her.

"No, I can't."

"And why not?"

"Because I need someone with a rooting interest, and that would be you."

"A personal question . . ." I wasn't asking permission. "Why did you leave him?"

She seemed a bit set back by the question and answered with a cliché. "I needed some space."

"You could have tried the *Yellow Pages*."

She had the ability to slough off sarcasm.

"Truth is, Alex had a pathological need for solitude. That's why he was a writer. You must understand some of that."

I did.

"Even when he wasn't alone, he was still alone." (I understood some of that, too.) "For the other person in the room it becomes unbearable. At least it did for me."

"Sorry I asked."

"It wasn't easy, and I never really did . . . leave him. I couldn't live with him, but I couldn't give him up. He had . . . substance."

"And what did you have?"

Her smile was not exactly withering but it did dry the air.

"I don't know. If you find him alive, ask him."

"Beauty, I'd say," which I did, making it sound like a curse.

As you can tell, I wasn't exactly crazy over Shelley. If I knew the other two wives I wouldn't be too crazy about them either. Let the man get lost in his own head, if he has to. Everybody comes out eventually, at least for visits. As long as the guy doesn't cheat on you or beat up on you, find a way, if you love him.

It wasn't a shadow; it was more like a presence that suddenly fell over us. Shelley looked up first. Sargeant Beckman was peering over the top of the free-standing bulkhead, taking in the nude portrait of the infamous redhead. He looked down at me and said, "Are you messing in my business? Say yes, I could use the help."

"Hey, everybody's got to eat. Shelley Lavendar, meet Sargeant Beckman, the fourth best cop in the Seattle Police Department."

Cop in the room. She seemed almost imperceptibly to recoil. Most people do something like that upon meeting a cop . Even I, back when I was a cop, used to tighten up when I saw a black-and-white in my rear-view mirror.

Beckman gave her some long eyes.

"Pleased to meet you, Sargeant Beckman."

"Likewise, I'm sure."

"Excuse me, Shelley."

I rose and walked to the other side of the bulkhead. I turned Beckman toward the bar and whispered, "Roll your tongue back in, Beckman, she's married. And, oh, so are you."

"She is a babe. Who is she?"

"Remember Alex Krapp, my screenwriter client?"

"The one who took off on his Harley and was never seen again?"

"That's the one. She's his wife."

"You mean widow, right? Hasn't the guy been declared dead?"

"Not by her, apparently. She wants me to find him."

"Good luck on that."

I nodded toward the galley entrance.

"You see that king salmon?"

He followed my nod and said, "Yeah, how can you miss it?"

"Alex Krapp caught it."

"Not around here."

"In Canada."

"Nice fish."

"He gave it to the owner. He used to hang out here before he disappeared."

"Yeah? So?"

"A dead man, my number on a matchbook from here, Alex's fish on the wall, and his wife suddenly calling me and wanting me to find a man who's been missing for nearly two years. It's all pretty strange, ain't?"

"Some things just bounce off each other like that."

"Yeah, well, there's more."

"More of what?"

"I just got a very unsettling text message," I told him, "less than an hour ago."

I opened my phone and held it in front of both of us. My mistake.

"Whoa," he said.

"Whoa what?"

"That's the screenwriter. Why do you have him as your wallpaper?"

Busted. I looked over at Shelley. She hadn't heard. I had no answer, not for Beckman or for myself. I put a picture of Alex on my phone the day I said good-bye to him. I don't know why, I just did, and it's still there.

"I have a picture of my kids for my wallpaper," said the cop. "Most people use pictures of their kids."

"My kid is grown up and in the navy."

"Oh, okay, so you can use the picture of someone else that you *love*."

"It's a free country."

"Quinn . . . is this healthy?"

"I don't know. I'll see the chaplain, okay? In the meantime, look."

I went to the text message, but he didn't look at it. He looked at me.

"Don't take the job, Quinn. I say this as a friend. This is not good for you."

"Yeah, all right, but this has nothing to do with that. Look, will you?"

He read the text.

"Who is this guy?"

"Which one?"

"Either one. Bruno or Stefano."

"I don't have a freaking clue. Your stiff wouldn't be named Stefano, would he? Or Steve?"

"He's still a John Doe. That's why I'm here."

"I'm not liking this."

"Dead again. Maybe this is someone from your reincarnation chat group."

I believe in reincarnation. It is not so much a belief as an acceptance. Given a choice, I'd take heaven, if I could have a short tour first. Beckman will occasionally beat me over the head with it. And he knows I'm not in any chat group.

"A dead man has my number; someone texts me that someone named Stefano has to die. A link? Duh?"

"And what does that have to do with your screenwriter and his fish and his hot wife and his picture on your *wallpaper*?"

"One thing at a time."

"So text him back, why don't you?"

"Text him back? And say what? 'Good idea, I never liked Stefano anyway?'"

"Ask him why this Stefano has to bite it."

"He expects me to know."

"Don't anticipate."

I looked back at Shelley. She was refreshing her makeup. So I texted Bruno a single word, "Why?"

I held the phone and looked at it.

"It may take a minute," Beckman said.

"I know that."

I shut the phone and put it away. I knew he wanted to grill me about the other thing, but I said, "Lars, this is Sargeant Beckman. He won't bite, and anyway he's had his shots."

Then I did an about-face and went back to Shelley and what was left of my herring, which I thought I would eat but found out I couldn't.

Six

I parked the PT in my building's underground parking and walked back up the ramp to the alley, Shelley's duffel slung over my shoulder. Emerging on Yesler, I saw my three Indians camped out under the pergola, so I detoured up to the Korean store on the corner and bought a liter of Pepsi and three ham-and-cheese sandwiches. On my way to the office I laid them on the boys.

"Hey, you're all right, Quinn," said Clifford Everybodytalksabout. "Not much to look at, but you're all right."

Not the first time he said that.

"How's business?" asked the third one. One of these days he will tell me his name.

"I'm sifting through my offers."

"Us too," mumbled David Hidesbehindthesmoke, around his sandwich. "We're torn between go to hell, get a job, or fuck off."

"Remember the man on the Harley Road King?" I asked them.

"Rest in peace, bro'," said Clifford.

"Your one true love," mumbled David.

"See, now, I didn't know that about you," I said. "I would have thought you had no imagination at all."

"He sees things. In dreams," said the third one.

"Well, leave me out of them."

"What about the old biker?" said Clifford.

"His wife wants to hire me."

"What for?"

"To find out if maybe he's still alive."

"Whoa. Sounds like a serious obligation to me."

In other words, something to be avoided.

"He is still alive, definitely," said he-who-dreams.

"So why haven't you told me that before, if you're so sure he's my one true love?"

"It never came up."

"Hey, you hear about the dead soldier on Alaskan Way this mornin'?" asked Clifford.

"I was there," I said. "He was dead. Definitely."

"Murdered, right?"

"Oh yeah."

I didn't get into the other unsettling details.

"You gonna take the job?"

"What job?"

"Findin' the old Harley rider."

"He wasn't that old," I said, a little annoyed with myself for even having that kind of conversation with these lushes.

"Who was the dead guy on Alaskan Way?"

"John Doe," I said. "Nobody Iknows his name."

"I know," said the dreamer and he went into a trance.

"Oh, shit," said I.

The other two laughed, at me or at him, I don't know. With his eyes closed, a half-eaten sandwich held aloft in one hand, David intoned, "He was the 'Rider in the Storm.'"

"The original? I thought it was 'Rider *on* the Storm,'" I said.

"I think it's 'Rider*s* on the Storm,'" said Clifford. "Plural."

His eyes still shut, David murmured, "There's a killer on the road; his brain is squirmin' like a toad."

"Sweet Jesus." I'd had enough for one sitting. "Later. Try to stay warm, okay? And, David? Toads don't squirm."

"Oh, yes, they do, ma'am. Everything squirms."

As I walked away to the side entrance of the Pioneer Building, where I had my office, Clifford yelled after me, "So are you gonna go look for the gone dude?"

"Don't know yet," I called back over my shoulder.

"Well, we're here for you, Quinn!"

"You'd be here anyway," I reminded them. "You're always here."

In my office, I separated the cassettes Shelley had marked apart from the big pile. I popped the one marked #1 into my recorder and put on the earphones.

The last words Alex spoke to me—I replay them often, whenever I'm in a certain mood—were in a sweet, quiet, and, I suppose, injured voice. Now on cassette #1 he sounded unhinged. He describes that day, when he left from Pioneer Square, riding through Georgetown toward the freeway, and encountering a group of kids spilling out of some all-night rave. He rambled on about once going to a rave himself, on research, but finding nothing of drama or comedy or anything more useful to him than color in transition. He said that bit of research cost him the upper tones in his right ear and bought him some occasional vertigo.

He should never have been on a motorcycle, I thought. I turned on my swivel chair and said to the brick wall, "Why did you have to ride off on that damned bike?"

When Krapp was the age of those kids, he said, he was home watching *Naked City* (and taking notes.) Or at the movies seeing *From Here to Eternity* for the third time, having his heart broken again for poor Prewitt, the bugler, his inspiration for enlisting, though he was smart enough to enlist in the navy. Or in his room reading "Hills Like White Elephants," a very short story about abortion, and his favorite Hemingway piece.

At the freeway entrance he made a random choice to go north despite the frigid weather. On Route 5, a movie idea came upon him, so he clamped a finger of his glove between his teeth and yanked. He reached into his jacket and pulled out the Olympus Pearlcorder. He flipped the visor of his helmet up and started recording, commenting to himself that this probably wasn't good motorcycling at eighty miles per hour.

"A young biker," I heard him say, "quintessentially without direction. An anti-hero. A pretty girl standing alone on a run-down street. He can read her. 'Sunday Morning Comin' Down' on the soundtrack. The girl is heroin thin, beautiful, but sad-eyed. Uma Thurman? No, way too old now. Somebody new. Whoever. The girl is waiting there, just waiting. For what? For someone to enter her life, anyone, someone who can make her feel something, anything. She sees the biker. Tentatively she raises her hand. Take me with you, I don't care where you're going. Cool existential stuff. All in the acting, no dialog yet. Today's audiences hate talk. A connection is made. He downshifts, does a U-turn, speeds back to her, pulls up to the curb, stops. The girl smiles. A tear worms out. She gets on the seat behind him, wraps her arms around him, and off they go, all before the credits. Good start, cute meet. Twenty years ago it might have worked. Naw, thirty years ago. A moment, and what is life but the moment?

I caught myself holding my breath, because of the edge on his voice and the sound of the traffic and the wind whipping him. I had known him one way, briefly, wanting the whole while to know him much better, and there I was, now, in his brain, where I had no right to be. I was relieved when he turned off his recorder. I turned off mine and went into the hallway, looking to see if there was anyone I knew, but the atrium was deserted. I had to go back to the office. I punched the play button. Alex was waiting to cross into Canada and it was quiet around him and he sounded a little more like I remembered him.

He talked about the weather, a cold drizzle, which he didn't seem to mind, as he waited in line at the border. He described that last little stretch of coastal road, the hidden Route 11, and how it gently twisted up to Bellingham, and how when he was on it he caught a rare and spectacular sunbreak.

Since the borders had been tightened, the lines were long and slow in each direction. He waited in the drizzle, his recorder running in his breast pocket, which must have been unzipped. Every time the line moved forward, he walked the bike between his legs, half-walking, half-wrestling, because, as he pointed out, the bike weighed eight hundred pounds. He actually talked to the bike at times, which he had named Minnie.

The Harley was named for Mickey Mouse's girlfriend because the Disney Studio purchased it for him, to settle a minor contractual dispute. Krapp's agent claimed that Disney owed him twenty thousand dollars for an additional rewrite done under duress. The studio, of course, claimed they owed him nothing, because technically it was a polish, not a rewrite. Apparently, these disputes are common and some way is found to work them out. In this case

Krapp said he would settle for a new motorcycle. Disney agreed, assuming the company would come out ahead. The bike he wanted, however, was a special edition 1994 Harley-Davidson Road King, which proved to be one of the motorwork's most popular models. Disney's team of professional negotiators came up against a heavily tattooed pipe fitter whose name was on the waiting list and might be enticed to let it go. At the end of the day the best they could do was twenty-eight thousand dollars.

Krapp finally got to the border gate and spoke to the guard.

"Citizenship?"

"Why not?" said Krapp vaguely.

"What is your citizenship, sir?"

"Oh, mine? U.S. I thought you were offering me citizenship. Which I would seriously consider, by the way. Bush has pretty much wrecked a good country."

The customs man went on flatly. "Place of residence?"

"Seattle. An island off Seattle."

"Purpose of your visit?"

"Ah . . . I'm not sure. Just laying low, really."

"How long will you be in Canada?"

"No idea."

There was a gap of silence. The guard was probably running the vitals through the computer.

After a moment, I heard the guard say, "Where will you be staying?"

"I hadn't thought about that."

Alex was directed to an area where he and the bike might be examined. A beagle did most of the work. Nothing illegal was sniffed out, but the sheer number of cassettes and tapes in the saddlebags must have given the authorities some pause.

"I'm a writer," I heard Krapp explain.

Another moment of dead air, and then, "You're free to go. Enjoy your stay in Canada."

"Frankly," Krapp said, "I think this was a mistake. Not yours. Mine. I should have gone south."

Were I in the audience, I might have chuckled at this little scene. Alone in my office, I teared up.

Seven

Half an hour into Happy Hour, with an hour and a half to go, I hauled into Brasa and out of the fierce wet wind. Suki saw me heading toward the bar and started building my sapphire-blue martini. By the time I draped my parka and babushka over the back of the bar stool, my drink was sitting in front of me, all pure and inviting.

"Hey, Quinn."

"Hey, Suki."

"You eating tonight?"

"I hope so. Remind me."

I numbed my lips with the icy wonder of gin kissed by vermouth and sounded by an olive. Nothing was wrong in my world at that moment.

Still, Alex's voice lodged in my head, first edgy and unhinged, then calm and contemplative, as I remembered. I knew back then that he probably never had it in him to be a happy man—but a certain contentment must have settled over him, thanks to the phenomenon known as Danny, that time I came into his life. Remembering all that brought me down. If he's dead, he's dead. If he's not, he doesn't want to be found. And if I did try to find him, would I be doing it for Shelley or for myself? Would I be able to keep myself out of it? Did I want to, even? Were the past two years just waiting to get to this point?

I raised my head from the crystal ball my martini glass had become and saw Sargeant Beckman standing beside me.

"You drinking to forget?" he asked.

"I forgot."

"Mind if I join you?"

"Sit."

Beckman sometimes comes into Brasa, but usually when he knows I'll be there. He gave his best smile to Suki and ordered a Jack Daniels on the rocks.

"Anything shaking with your John Doe?" I asked him.

"No, but he's as much yours as mine, isn't he?"

"How do you figure?"

"You're the only connection. He had your number. And then there's all that other stuff."

"A lot of people have my number. Numbers get around. Freakin' Bruno has my number."

"Did he ever call you?"

"Bruno?"

"No, John Doe."

"I told you. If he ever called me I'd probably know his name."

"But Bruno did. Call you."

"I don't know Bruno either."

"So why's he sharing secrets with you?"

"What secrets?"

"Oh, about how Stefano must die."

"Is this an interrogation? 'Cause it's killing my buzz."

"Just a couple of friends talking over the day. It's been quite a day."

"If I had any connection with all of this, any stake in it at all, would I be running to you with that text message?"

"I don't know, you're kind of a smart babe."

"Exactly. Trust me, Beckman, I have nothing to do with Bruno, Stefano, or your John Doe."

"Maybe you do but you just don't know how you fit into it."

"Fair enough. Find out and tell me."

My phone dinged, and of course I jolted. It was another text message. I read it and said, "Speak of the devil. It's old Bruno."

The message was: "R U being coy?"

I showed it to Beckman. "Well, are you?" he asked.

"I'm glad you think this is funny."

I took a substantial hit off my martini. Beckman ordered a second drink and said, "Go ahead, text him back."

"And say what?"

"Whatever. Get him to say something more."

I typed as well as I could: "Stefano who?" Then I sucked up what was left of my martini, hoping this would be a short exchange because once on the second martini my texting skills, never good to begin with, take a serious skid, which might account for why I got the original message. Maybe Bruno was into the sauce himself. I sent the message and ordered another martini.

"Don't forget to eat something," Suki told me.

"Right. I'll have the Moroccan steak sandwich."

"Sounds good," said Beckman.

"Join me," said I.

"Can't. Princess Di is expecting me for dinner."

His wife's name was Diana.

"How did it go with Lars at The Copper Gate?" I asked.

"Nothing. I showed him a picture of the John Doe but it didn't ring any bells. I left the Polaroid so he could show it to the other bartender and to the owner and maybe a couple regulars. He said he would. Maybe we'll get a hit on fingerprints or DNA."

"What you look like after you've been beat up and shot in the back of the head isn't always what you used to look like," I observed.

"Beat up isn't the half of it. When we stripped down the John Doe, it became pretty clear the dude'd been tortured."

"Get out!"

"In the classical sense. Cigarette burns, cuts, etcetera, etcetera."

"Woi Yesus."

"Indeed, whatever that means."

I sipped on my second martini and looked down at the silent phone. "How do you feel about running Bruno down?"

"I thought you'd never ask."

I asked Suki for a book of matches and wrote down the number from my recent call list. I paused midway and Beckman and I looked at each other, like, this is the way it happens. You call for a matchbook, you write down a number, maybe you make a mistake, who can say where it will finally wind up? Maybe in a dead man's pocket. I handed the matchbook to Beckman.

He looked at the number and said, "This is a Verizon number."

"You can tell?"

"Yeah. I'll give them a call."

He drained his second drink and stood up, reaching for his cash.

"Suki," I said, "put that on my tab."

Not a minute after Beckman left Brasa, I got another text from Bruno. I almost ran outside to call him, but worried I might trip and do a header. The message: "Don't be cute."

Eight

I heard the drum, I heard the singer, but I thought it must have been a dream. On any given night, middle of the night, the tribals might wake me up with their sad and futile attempts to recapture The Song, the key to their once proud existence, with two of them reaching for the rhythm of the drum on overturned city trash containers or jettisoned five-gallon plastic pails or empty Office Depot boxes, while the singer tortures himself for the release of chants he knows are in him somewhere, deep down in the blood. It was like one of those nights. I'm naked, arid, with a failed ecosystem in my mouth, making my way to the faucet and twisting my head under it until I can gulp no more and then letting the water rush over my face.

Toweling off, I stumble to the window to yell down my customary threats, or just to listen, to cheer them on internally, but they are not singing or drumming. They are deep into their sleeping bags under the pergola. Some view. Why do I even live here? What's so hot about this condo that makes it list for six-fifty? I was there mostly out of ennui. I'd found the place the first day I got into town, still reeling from the shock of divorce and the sense of failure it leaves you with. I was putting behind me a comfortable three-bedroom, three-bath house overlooking the Spokane River Gorge, built before those developments started popping up along the North Indian Trail, a house that used to be a blessed refuge from the streets I worked daily as a cop. Granted, I didn't know that Pioneer Square turns into Bourbon Street every weekend, but by the time I realized it I didn't care. I had made myself a nest. My little urban enclosure was a comfort to me, even if I did have to rouse occasionally some drunk on the nod blocking the entrance on First Avenue. It was *my* place, all mine. I didn't cook anymore. I didn't entertain drugstore people, including the one who stole my husband. I didn't entertain anybody but myself. In the more than three years I'd lived in the condo, I let only two people inside, both men, one now dead, the other either dead or missing. I have no plans to entertain anyone else. This is *my* place. Until I have to move. Unless I buy it myself, if even I can.

Awake now, I knew I was looking at two, three hours of worrying about hearing things and my wrecked relationships and the state of real estate. I put on my earphones and slid another one of Krapp's cassettes into my player. I sat at the window with my notepad.

Having turned his motorcycle around in Canada, Alex Krapp headed down to the Olympic Pennisula, winding up wet, cold, and tired at the Lodge at Lake Quinault, where he asked for the best room they had. That would be the one where you couldn't hear the couple next door fucking.

Alex: "I wonder if listening to people fuck next door can really induce psychosis, as that neurotic director once told me. He sounded pretty sure."

Alex called Shelley.

"Hey, remember that narration in *Blade Runner?*"

"Alex? Where are you, sweetheart?"

The tenderness of her voice stung me. She'd hardened a bit since then, but who hasn't?

"Remember that time, years after, when I met Harrison Ford for the first time and he told me he hated the narration and deliberately gave it his least, which is very little indeed, over dinner at Jackson Hole, and we had a good laugh about it, and the director, who could hardly eat because he had his face pressed so hard against Harrison's butt, would say whenever Harrison was out of earshot, 'That animal, we have to work with that animal . . .'?"

"Why are you doing this?"

"What?"

"Try remembering how nice it was to go up to Wyoming in a private jet and to be paid ridiculously much," said Shelley.

"I've told you this story, haven't I?"

"Oh, sweetheart, you're doing it again."

"Repeating myself?"

"You know what I mean. Just don't go there. Where are you right now?"

"Simple questions like that lately strike me as so profound."

"Let's try to keep it simple, honey."

"Where am I? Ahead of myself, that's where I always am, even when I try so hard to catch up. I'm on the bike."

"Are you taping this?"

"Yeah, why?"

"Do you have to?"

"I guess."

"Life happens, whether you tape it or not."

"Prove it."

"But you're not on the bike this minute?"

"No, I'm at Lake Quinault. You hear that?"

"No, what?"

"Geese honking overhead. You have to *hear* to be *here.*"

"Tell me what it's like."

"Well, I'm between the lake and the rain forest, in a canopy of red cedars, douglas firs, and hemlocks. Thick with ferns and moss and wild mushrooms. They say there are cougars."

"So you're going to take the Olympia loop back up to the island?"

"No, I want to ride some more, farther south, find some sun."

"Come down here, it's in the seventies. You can kick back and relax."

"Okay. Thanks. I will. It's a date. I'm just laying low for a while, not that anyone down there will even notice."

"Oh, sweetheart, they don't have to notice."

"You're okay for money, aren't you?"

"Don't be silly. I'm loaded."

"Because maybe I don't need those hundred-grand-a-week re-write jobs anymore."

"That's always been up to you."

"Or the meetings with Sean Penn or Ron Howard on their pet projects. Or those conferences on how to crack the Siamese twin story, or the *How Mars Was Won* story, or the *Master and Marguerita* adaptation. You still there?"

"I'm here."

"Would I miss, like, poker with Al Pacino, or shopping for bargain clothes with Dustin in lower Manhattan, or walks with Harrison on his ranch?"

"Was it all that much fun anyway?"

"Shelley, the only fun it ever was was telling you about it."

"There's something I never told you."

"Oh, shit, here it comes."

"No, nothing like that. God. Is sex ever very far from your mind?"

"How would I know?"

"I've told you everything in that department."

"More than I needed to know, actually."

"Do you want to hear this or not?"

"Shoot."

"I went to a shrink a few times, when we were both down there."

"You never told me that."

"No, I couldn't."

"How'd it go?"

"She told me I should work on taking care of myself, because you were a screenwriter and you would never be happy. Most of her clients were screenwriters, so she knew."

"I was always happy making love to you. I was delirious."

I didn't need to hear that. Too late, it's been heard. I tried to blame the irrational clutch in my stomach on all that had happened that day. I missed the next few exchanges so I had to rewind the tape.

"That's such a short time in a person's life," she said.

"It was in ours."

"You know I still love you. I would do anything for you."

"I know."

The tape ran on but there were no words. Then, "Are you still recording this?"

"You know me. I'm looking for a good quote but all I can come up with is the old 'living well is the best revenge.'"

"Revenge against whom?"

"Who have you got?"

"Ah, *The Wild One*, right?"

"Screenplay by John Paxton, nineteen fifty-three, directed by Laslo Benedeck, produced by Stanley Kramer. Starring Marlon Brando, Lee Marvin, and Mary Murphy. The lines were: 'What are you rebelling against?' Brando says, 'What have you got?'"

"And yet you seem to have contempt for the movies."

"No, I have contempt for the audiences."

"Sweetheart, no one else cares whether you live well or not."

"You might be missing the point. I'd like to change everything. I'd like to learn something new. Sculpting, maybe. That might be a good medium for me."

"I think that's a wonderful idea."

"Or I could write my memoirs."

"Oh . . . I don't think that's a very good idea, sweetheart."

The cassette ran out. I turned toward the window, which was being pelted with rain, the kind of lateral rain we get up here. If I were Shelley, I thought, I wouldn't want another woman listening to a conversation like that. Unless it was a woman I suspected was in love with my husband.

Nine

My office is one room on the fifth floor of the Pioneer Building, with a plastic snake named Stanley on the window ledge scaring away pigeons. No secretary, no anteroom. If you're waiting to see me, you're waiting in the hall, under the atrium, sitting on a bench the management was kind enough to position there for just that purpose. On that bench, fhe following morning, waiting for me, was Shelley Lavendar, and she was a tad fretful.

"I tried to call you," she said, with something of an accusation that I wasn't readily enough available to her.

"I keep it on vibrate 'til I finish my morning latte. These days."

I didn't mention my Dance of the Startled Phonophobe.

"I called the office, too."

"Yeah, well obviously I wasn't here."

I unlocked the door and she followed me inside.

"I'm leaving town today," she said, "and I really have to hurry. You've heard about the fires?"

"What fires?"

"In Santa Barbara . . . Montecito . . . the whole area, it's all in flames. They're calling it the Tea Fire."

"Why?"

"There was an old place called the Tea House, an old café. That's where it started."

"I don't watch the evening news. It's too hard to sleep if you do."

"My neighbors are scrambling to get what they can before the evacuation order. God, it's devastating. I must get back."

"Isn't this what always happens in California, fires?"

"Not in November. You see, the planet's drying up."

I turned on the lights, put my latte on the desk, and hung my purse and parka on the hook.

"What do you hear from the neighbors?"

"I can't reach anybody. I have to go back and try to salvage what I can. It's horrible. I haven't slept all night."

She was distraught and growing more that way, but for someone who was up all night, she looked ready for close-ups, which was probably what made me ask, "Were you an actress ever?"

The question seemed to startle her. Maybe she was trying to forget the past, or at least that part of it.

"Not a very successful one, I'm afraid."

"Were you in any of Alex's movies?"

"No, but that's how we met, at an audition for one of his movies." She smiled, remembering.

"And you didn't get the part?"

"No, the director wanted to '. . . go in a different direction.'"

"But not the writer. Apparently."

"Yes, I lost the role but I got the writer."

Which I always understood was not exactly the best way for a girl to get ahead in Hollywood.

"And you're here, why?" I asked, getting back to business.

I probably sounded colder than I intended. Though I wasn't in love with her, I could have shown her a little compassion. The lady lost her husband, after all, and now her house might be burning down.

"I'm anxious to have you start, obviously. Have you listened to the cassettes?"

"A couple."

"Were they helpful?"

"If I were trying to find out what happened to Alex? Not too."

"But you have to listen to the others. There has to be something in them, something that gives a clue to where he is . . . or what happened to him."

"Last night I listened to the phone conversation you had with him, when he called from Lake Quinault."

"Yes?"

"Was that the last time you talked to him?"

"It was."

"I'm a little surprised you would want me to hear that."

"It's not that I *wanted* you to hear it. I *needed* you to hear it."

"Because it made me think you had a complicated relationship."

"Aren't they all?"

She had me there. Each in its own way. She didn't seem in such a big hurry anymore. She slipped down into herself. This was difficult for her, I knew. Whatever complications she had had with Alex, she obviously needed to see him again, if he was alive, or know what happened to him, if he wasn't.

"So . . . ," she said, "how will this work?"

"I don't think it will."

"What?"

"I can't help you."

"But you have to. You're my only hope."

"There are sixty PI's in Seattle, and more where you come from."

"Maybe, but only one of them was in love with Alex."

"Whoa! I told you, I didn't even know him all that well."

"I read your book."

"Did it say I loved him in the book?"

"You never gave yourself the permission."

"Look, don't try getting into my head. Listening to the cassettes only reminded me of how little I really knew him. You said you thought Alex might still be alive. I *always* thought that. He's running away, from three broken marriages, a profession he came to consider superfluous, from lies and deceit, from heartbreak. In short, from other people. He took it on the arfy-darfy. He's gone, get used to it. Maybe he's happy now."

"He can't be gone, not forever."

"Sure he can."

Once again, she fell down into herself, looking for an answer. What did she come up with? "He never said good-bye." Which put the cuffs on me. Sympathy for the other woman, all that. He did, after all, say good-bye to me, even if it was on one of his cassettes. She got to me, but not deep enough. I leaned back in my chair and looked at my latte.

"He was not just another client to you," she said.

"Maybe he wasn't, to begin with, but that's how it wound up. Just another client."

"I don't believe that. You *cared* for him."

I saw her tears welling up.

"I don't care much about anything," I said. "It's easier that way."

"Who are you trying to convince?"

"I'm sorry. Good luck on your house. Really."

"Please. I'm begging you. You have to find Alex, or find out what happened to him. I have to know. Please."

"He's been gone for nearly two years. Why the sudden urgency?"

She took a moment.

"Someone sent me those cassettes, the cassettes that were with him on that damned bike. If it wasn't Alex, it was someone who knows what's happened to him. If anyone can find out, it's you. You're the best detective in Seattle."

"I wish."

"Don't you even want to know if he's still alive?"

Now I took a moment.

"Tell me," she said, taking advantage of my hesitation, "how little you care about Alex."

When I didn't respond, she took her checkbook out of her purse and wrote a check. She laid it on the desk. I leaned forward and looked at it without touching it. I had to search for the comma to make sure. It was way too much. Okay, he was the lady's husband and maybe she loved him to pieces, and certainly she was rich, but the check was way too heavy. She could have hired a *firm* of investigators and still had enough left over for a long weekend in Palm Springs.

Blame it on my having grown up in an impoverished mining town. I still find myself shamefully motivated by money. At least it's helpful to think so.

"This is too much," I said, this time aloud, still not touching that check.

"I'm trying to impress upon you how important this is to me."

"I'm impressed."

"Then you'll do it?"

I thought of all the reasons why I shouldn't. A total of one. Then I thought of all the reasons I should. The same one, plus a lot of cash.

"It's got to be at my own speed, my own methods."

"Of course."

"In other words, don't call me, I'll call you."

"Absolutely." She smiled, dabbing her eyes with a hankie. "You have free rein. Thank you, Quinn." I could see on her face relief, hope, and a certain satisfaction that she tipped me over. "You'll never know how much this means to me."

In fact, I would.

"Now I really have to fly," she said.

I came from behind the desk and opened the door for her. She cornered me and gave me a squeezy girlfriend hug and an air kiss, neither of which I wanted or particularly enjoyed, but I guess it was in her nature. It's not in mine.

She was out of the office and heading toward the elevator when she spun around and said, "Oh, I forgot. Those cassettes you have, from before, you said you have twenty?"

"About twenty."

"May I have them, please?"

"Sure. You mean, now?"

"If you don't mind."

"I don't mind, but I'm not sure . . . they're around here somewhere."

"Could you look?" she said.

"Don't you have a plane to catch?"

"I have a few minutes."

I pretended to look for them in my file cabinets, taking my time, even though I knew they were in my bottom desk drawer. I looked back over my shoulder at her. She seemed composed.

"I think they're in storage," I said. "Yeah, I remember. They were with some other boxes I put in storage."

"Where is your storage unit?"

In the parking garage below the condos, across the street, but I didn't tell her that. I said the unit was in Lynnwood and the key was around here somewhere. I told her that I would find the key and dig out the cassettes next time I was in Lynnwood and send them to her.

"When might that be?" she asked.

"You know, I listened to all of them. They were made long before he took off, of him and his conversations with Danny."

"All Danny?"

"All of them."

"All right, but legally they do belong to me and I'd like to have them."

"You will, but do you need them right this minute?"

She hesitated and said, "No, not this minute. But soon, before they're forgotten."

"I said I'd get them to you. I'll get them to you."

She looked like she didn't believe me.

After she left, I put the cassettes she wanted into a waste-basket liner and took them to Bernard's office. I opened the door and found him, as usual, on the phone promising someone that his tickets would put the guy so close to the field he'd be in danger of getting trampled by Maurice Morris.

Bernard used to be an LA crip, street name Romeo, now on the arfy-darfy himself, making an honest if not lavish living as a ticket scalper. His old homies probably wonder if *he* is alive or dead, but no one was paying a PI beaucoup bucks to find out. He signaled me to take a seat, but I put my bag on his desk and waited. He made the sale.

"Yo, yo, Quinn, this is all too easy, man, and you don't even have to pack."

"I'm happy for you, Bernard."

"Whaddaya need? I got two for *Wicked*. Oh, I forgot, you don't like musical comedy."

"More than I like football. No, I need you to hold this bag for me, like, under lock and key?"

He took the open end of the bag in his hands and looked up at me, like, may I? I nodded.

He looked inside the bag, then back up at me.

"Anybody willing to kill for these?"

"They're just cassettes, one man's ramblings about his life."

"So why do they need protection?"

"They probably don't. It's just that a particular lady seems a little too eager to have them."

Ten

"I need a physical destination, a place on the map, like New Orleans in *Easy Rider*. Which was kind of a stupid picture, actually, if you think about it. What I need is a definite place to go, and a purpose . . . wait one damn minute . . . why do I? It's a spiritual destination! I won't know where it is until I've arrived!"

I was listening to Alex, back in his unfamiliar, ragged voice, talking to himself as he rode his bike south. I'd been at it for most of the morning. It wasn't exactly easy listening.

He swerved to miss a crow picking at some road kill and that prompted him to talk about Carlos Castaneda, whom he knew personally, turning into a crow to complete a sorcerer's task. He talked about the society of crows, which is said to be highly evolved. He talked about once actually witnessing a crow court in the park convicting and banishing a defendant for some crow crime unknowable to man.

He rode his bike through Aberdeen, an ugly little logging town, talking about Kurt Cobain, who might have been happy there, a grungy youngster in a garage putting together the band, determined to push the music further than it's ever been, resolved never to sell out to the hideous entertainment industry, to skirt around it, to avoid getting any of it on him. And then . . . and then, so soon after, sprawled dead on the floor of his Seattle home, the guest house actually, in case the family wanted to continue living in the main house, and then Courtney Love snipping some of his pubic hair as a keepsake, which—"O, the horror!"—is destined someday to come up for sale on e-Bay.

(By the way, and this is me, there once was a Seattle mayoral candidate whose entire platform was the promise to uncover the conspirators from the music industry who murdered Kurt Cobain and tried to make it look like a suicide. Back to the cassette.)

Alex Krapp rode past Cape Disappointment through a light drizzle, leaving Washington behind and rising up and over the bridge to Astoria, portal to Oregon, across the mighty Columbia River. Out of Astoria, he pounded the Oregon coast, nothing to slow him down but a little fog and rain, because all the Good Neighbor Sams and their behemoth rigs were in storage or Tucson.

He caught himself feeling almost happy, twist after turn, stopping only for a pee against a tree, some rehydration, then kneading his ass with both hands to get some feeling back. He rode all the way to Eureka, California, and fell exhaused into bed at the first motel he came upon.

Over breakfast in the morning, at an unnamed cafe, he talked about meeting with Bob Dylan a couple times, exploring doing one of Dylan's songs as a film.

"Why Dylan wanted to get into the movies is a mystery to me. I mean, I can see the studio meeting after the first draft: Dylan, the studio v-p, her assistant, and the 'Creative Team.' The v-p would say, 'We love this first draft. Great start! We think the characters are super, generally. The pace is almost there already, even though it sags in the second act. The visuals will be terrific, with a little tweaking. Really, we have only a few notes. Like the opening. *Once upon a time* is a cliché. This isn't a fairy tale. Our target demographic is the young adult. We'd like to start right in with the action, something going on right away.'

"Then someone else would say: 'We're a little concerned about the chorus, that constant pounding of *How does it feel?* It seems unnecessarily vindictive. We think that without changing the language at all, just the tone, we can make that a statement of concern. He's genuinely worried about her, what her future will be. It makes him more sympathetic.'

"The v-p jumps in: 'We all love the rolling-stone image. That goes on the poster!'

"The assistant sees an opening: 'Some of the language is confusing. I mean, a lot of it is . . .'

"Another team member doesn't let her finish: 'Well, I really like *vacuum of his eyes*.'

"The third doofus needs to score so he says: 'Yeah, but what about . . . *frowns on the jugglers and the clowns*? . . . What's that all about? The circus is so last century. And . . . *juiced in it*? . . . I know what you're trying to say but nobody will know what that means. *Wasted*, maybe. *Fucked up* would be better.'

"'I'm bothered by the diplomat and his Siamese cat. Too oblique and it's just one more budget item. We're doing this for a price and we could easily lose the cat wrangler. Why can't the guy have something like a facial tic instead of a Siamese cat?'

"'I like that she might be invisible. Could be great, but when you say she has no secrets to reveal, what secrets are you talking about? You have to let the audience in on the secrets.'"

"'Could we talk about *Napoleon in rags and the language that he used*? First of all, I don't know what that means. I know who Napoleon is but most of the audience won't. How does it relate to the same bum that she gives a dime? Is he a homeless person? And what language *is* he speaking? Is it French?'"

The cassette goes on until it runs out, about this imagined meeting, but you get the idea. Okay, I could have skipped over most of this. I *am* skipping over most of it now, in telling it, but I didn't know when or where he might say the thing that pointed me in the right direction. So indulge me.

I slipped in another cassette.

"Whew! Okay, I've backed down to eighty miles per hour, on the way to Ukiah, after running a hundred, hundred and ten miles per hour, fast as I've ever pushed Minnie but she doesn't seem to mind. *I'm* a nervous wreck."

Which in my mind pushed the notion that he might have, indeed, finally killed himself on that bike.

"Even at those speeds, she's right behind me on her little Sportster, like the demon she aspires to be, like the shadow of death that Carlos once conjured for me. She's got no more protecting her than a beanie helmet and her colors. In the twisties she could have overtaken me but she hung back. Then on the straightaways there she is again beside me, sharing the same lane, looking over at me and smiling, and me with white knuckles. Carlos once warned me that death is always just over your left shoulder, barely out of sight, edging closer and closer, sometimes dropping back, sometimes coming abreast so that you can catch glimpses of his hooded head, and then ultimately overtaking you no matter how fast you run. But you run anyway."

I stopped the cassette. I knew I must have skipped something. Where did the girl on the motorcycle come from? I tried a couple of others and found what I thought was the right one.

It was morning. Krapp left Route 101 and rode in third gear along the Avenue of the Giants, through massive, heroic redwoods. He pulled off at a souvenir shop and had a cup of coffee next to a wooden statue of Paul Bunyan. He was wondering about the road not taken, what he might have become, for better or worse.

The lids of both saddlebags were open and he was kneeling next to the bike, sorting through spilled tapes with growing frustration, looking for that particular moment some thirty years before. Why, he asked himself aloud, did he ever even bother to bring along any of those old standard-size cassettes? Utterly useless since he didn't bring a recorder capable of playing them.

"*Fox lot, no guts.* That sounds like it. Found, but still lost. What's this? *MJ in P*? Has to be Mick Jagger in Paris. A movie actually came out of that, a hackneyed movie that audiences refused to inflict upon themselves, and a movie without my name on it, thank God! and without Jagger in it, because Mick was nothing if not smart enough to know when to cut and run, though he hedged his bet a little with a producer and a story credit, just in case. No one ever really knows if a picture, even though you hate it, will become wildly successful.

"In Mick's apartment, on the Ile de la Cite, the rangy Texan on her way out to a shoot in Milan, and the trashy little French bird Michele in to take her place, Mick played some cuts from the new album, still in post production . . . *I'm just waiting for a lady . . . I'm just waiting for a friend* . . . all the while chicken-dancing around the cold, threadbare living room, and at the same time reading the *Financial Times,* propped open on the ugly, tattered French sofa, still at the same time brain-storming his idea for a movie.

"The night before, smoking weed and emptying out the mini-bar in Taft's suite. He'd be dead in five years, of AIDS, poor guy. I think he wound up directing the picture himself because no real director would touch it. I'd come very close to wetting my pants listening to Mick do his voices, especially the little girls. We fell down on the floor laughing and when we picked ourselves up there was a riveting moment Jagger and I stood nose to nose, except that I was a good bit taller. I thought at that moment Mick Jagger was going to try to kiss me. Taft had warned me he sometimes did that to macho types. But instead Mick broke the moment by saying, 'I really like your suit.' It was that brown Pendleton, rugged, very Hemingwayesque. Wish I still had it."

I heard on the cassette the unmistakable rumble of a Harley-Davidson. It sounded as though it went by, turned around, and came back. Then the engine was cut and I heard a woman's voice say, "Havin' trouble?"

"Well, I could use a regular cassette player, not a mini."

"I have one."

"You don't."

"Here."

"I'm amazed. The magic of the road. Needs are somehow met."

"It's just a Walkman."

"*Just* a Walkman? It's an antique, found nowhere else except under this redwood."

"Knock yourself out."

"It might take a few minutes."

"Take your time."

"Hey, you're flying colors. Devil Dolls, San Francisco. Are you an outlaw?"

"Are you?"

"Maybe. But colorless."

"I'll just lie down here for a while. I've been riding all night."

"Wow. Take a nap."

Then I heard another voice, the voice that was Alex's many years before.

"In my car . . . just sitting . . . on the New York street, Fox lot . . . in my new used Mercedes, wanting so badly to turn the key, start up, drive away, leave everything, drive down into Mexico, disappear, embrace oblivion in some village too small to be on the map."

Thirty years ago, and he wanted to escape then.

I leaned forward in my chair. This might be the key to what I was looking for.

"How much longer can I spend ten hours a day, hour off for his psychiatrist, agonizing over every simple line of dialog, each of the one hundred and thirty pages tacked to the corkboard wall of his office, covered with scribblings and arrows and dialog encircled in little clouds, like comic-book conversations, which maybe they are becoming. What's happening? Am I a willing participant? . . . Am I standing last in line at the gang rape of my own wife?"

I heard the Walkman shut off. The mini recorder continued.

"What difference would it have made, really?"

"I'm sorry?"

"They would have brought in another writer, they owned the fucking script, they could do whatever they wanted to it. They could wipe their well-fed asses with it. And, look, I had a hundred thousand dollars. I paid off my mortgage before my father paid off his. I even had a little fuck-you money left over. Problem was I never said fuck you. I had a wife and a child, you see. And, hey, this was a major studio and an A-list director and some interest from Jack Nicholson."

"Jack Nicholson?"

"Yeah, it was a time when every producer claimed interest from Jack Nicholson. Now I guess it's Tom Cruise, who by the way got his first break in one of my movies. So what?"

"You're in the movies? What're you doing way up here, on a Road King?"

"I wish I knew. I write for the movies. I used to think that was something. It's not anything. And you?"

"I pierce skin."

"Well, that's something. You do it, you leave a hole."

"I share a parlor with a tattoo artist in North Beach. Slave to the Needle, it's called."

"Sounds inviting. You have a good voice."

"I've been told that."

"You could get voiceover work."

"I already got work."

"Actually, it turned out to be true."

"What did?"

"The interest from Jack Nicholson. He was directing his first picture then. A disaster. Everybody wants to direct. Everybody but me. I never wanted to direct."

"How come?"

"At best, a director is no more than a strong and sincere father to a large dysfunctional family. At worst, he's an inept father, an abusive father."

"Like mine."

"My sympathies."

"So it's all like, what, a family?"

"In the family that makes a movie, I'm the son they hide in the attic."

"What's with the cantaloupe?"

"I bought it this morning at a fruit stand. They didn't have any bananas. You want to share it?"

The tape went dead for a few moments. I pictured Alex cutting up a canteloupe. I wanted to fast forward, to see where this was going. It occurred to me that if and when I ever found the missing screenwriter, I would find him with a woman. Maybe even this woman. Maybe in Mexico.

Alex: "Cantaloupe is the best thing you can put in your mouth."

Devil Doll: "Second best."

"What could be better?"

"Pussy."

(Not with this woman.)

Alex: "You ever eat the other one?"

Devil Doll: "It's okay. You?"

"God, no. I'm a hopeless heterosexual."

"I don't discriminate sexually."

(She's back in the running.)

"Where were you heading when you ran into me?"

"North. Just ridin'."

"From San Francisco?"

"Yeah. I had a difficulty there. You?"

"South from Canada. I had a difficulty too. But it's turning into research for my memoir. I guess you'll be in it now."

"No problem."

"How old are you?"

"Twenty."

"That's pretty young for a Devil Doll."

"How old are you?"

"Pretty old, for a screenwriter. You want to ride together for a while?"

"Where?"

"I don't care."

"Awesome."

Eleven

Half a day on the case and what did I know for sure? The screenwriter met a twenty-year-old bisexual biker girl south of Eureka and they rode together, direction Ukiah. It's even money they went all the way to San Francisco, headquarters of the Devil Dolls, not to be confused with Dykes on Bikes. The police and CHP investigation at the time ended in Half Moon Bay, where Krapp last used his credit card to buy gas. Half Moon Bay is just south of San Francisco. That's pretty much all I knew for sure. Was he still with the Devil Doll? If not, did he tell her where he was going? I had no idea if the cops ever talked to her. Since they didn't have the cassettes, they wouldn't have known about her, so she would have had to come forward with whatever information she had, and that presupposes she read newspapers and knew that Krapp was missing, not a sure assumption; missing screenwriters don't get that much ink anyway. Krapp had talked to Shelley and indicated he would visit her, and he was certainly heading in that direction. He would have had to gas up again, maybe twice before he got there, but after Half Moon Bay he could have paid cash. One thing was certain: he never got to Shelley's house in Santa Barbara. Whatever happened to Alex Krapp happened between Half Moon Bay and Santa Barbara, a gap of two hundred and fifty-eight miles, as the crow flies. As I thought about it I realized that even that wasn't certain. I was a bit distrustful of Shelley. Maybe he *did* show up in Santa Barbara and for some reason she was keeping that to herself. I was going to have to start with the Devil Doll.

Online, I found the number to Slave to the Needle on Columbus Street in San Francisco. I dialed it up. A man of few social skills answered.

"Speak."

"My name is Quinn . . ."

"Yeah?"

". . . and I'm a private investigator in Seattle."

"Okay."

"I'm trying to locate a woman who does piercings. Does she share your space?"

"Nobody shares my space."

"I meant your store, the tattoo place, not, you know, your personal space."

"Piercings are done here."

"By whom?"

"Who are you looking for?"

"I don't know her name, but . . ." I had the sense the phone went against his chest while he tipped off the Devil Doll to the call. "Hello?" Nothing. Then he came back on.

"Who are you looking for?"

"Probably the person you were just talking to."

"You want a piercing?"

"No, I want to talk to the girl who does piercings. She rides a Harley Sportster and belongs to the Devil Dolls Motorcycle Club. Is she there?"

"She only does appointments."

"I just need to ask her a few questions."

"Like I said."

I gave the yonko my number and asked him to have the Devil Doll call me. Fat chance.

I took the elevator down to the square and walked across Cherry Street and up to Bakeman's, the underground sandwich shop, where it's always the day after Thanksgiving: roasted turkey sandwiches, carved from the bird, with cranberry sauce. I fell into line, and three cops fell in behind me, all of us trying to keep up with the rapid-fire questions of the girls building the sandwiches. I ordered four, one for me and three to take back to my Indians.

I sat alone at a table where I could look out the windows and see the feet of the passing pedestrians.

Halfway through my sandwich, I had a little jolt from my cell phone. Another text message. Bruno again.

"Can you b-liv that sob?"

I texted back: "What sob?"

It took only a moment: "D'uh? Stefano! Do dat, he got 2 B got!"

I tried to call him and just talk this out, but it went right to message. I hung up. Bruno, it seemed, preferred to communicate by text messages.

Out of Bakeman's, I walked across the street on my way to delivering the sandwiches to the pergola. I wanted to drop in at the Mystery Bookshop. I don't do that often enough, and they don't know me that well there. I kind of feel I don't belong, but that's my problem. I'm working on it.

Neither J.B. nor Sandy was there, probably out to lunch. There was a new kid in charge. I introduced myself.

"Wow, what a coincidence!" he said. "I sold your book last week."

"It happens."

"Man comes in and asks for an advance copy."

"What? You mean the new one?"

"Yeah, I told him it wouldn't be out 'til March but he really wanted it right away. I go, we don't sell advance copies, but he offered me fifty bucks for it, so I dug it out and sold it to him." I was stunned. "Was that wrong?" he asked.

"Why would somebody pay fifty bucks for an advance proof of a paperback worth fourteen bucks?"

"Book people are funny. They collect all kinds of stuff."

"Regular customer, new guy, what?"

"Never saw him before. Spoke with a German accent."

"Would his name be Bruno?"

"I don't know, he paid cash."

"What did he look like?"

"Well, if you looked up *German gentleman* in Wikipedia, there'd probably be a picture of this guy. Fair skinned, blond hair, square jaw, tight lips, wore a suit and tie, a nice charcoal-gray overcoat, and a fedora. Looked like a young Republican."

"How young?"

"Twenty-something. Didn't say much, all business. Wanted your book, and when he had it, he boogied."

Bruno is a German name. Bruno doesn't like to speak on the phone, prefers texting, maybe so I wouldn't know he was German. Then why would he tell me his name was Bruno? He could have just as easily said Sam-I-am. I really didn't know what to make of it.

I made my way to the pergola where I had to stir my Indians out of their collective stupor and force feed them. At least I had to sit with them and make sure they ate.

Clifford asked, "Did they find out who killed that cowboy yesterday?"

"Or even who that killed cowboy was?" David added.

I'd forgotten about all of that. Then I remembered that the John Doe was shot with a German Luger. A man with a German accent paid too much for an advance copy of my book about Alex Krapp. A man with a German name keeps texting me about killing Stefano. Could a piece of strudel be far behind?

Still sitting with the Indians, I text-messaged Bruno: "U like 2 read?"

I went back up to my office and put in a call to my editor in New York. I left a voice mail asking him to check the advance list for the new book. Did it include a Shelley Lavendar from Santa Barbara?

By that time Bruno texted back with his answer: "I prefer TV."

I called Beckman.

"I don't know what to do about this Bruno creep," I said. "He won't talk to me but he keeps texting me about murder."

"I was just going to call you about that."

"You got something?"

"Bruno's using a cheap no-contract phone, pre-paid for twenty hours air time. It was activated by Verizon in the name of Baron Von Rothschild."

"C'mon!"

"He gave a Starbucks in Bellevue as his address."

"Da frick."

"The phone was sold by an independent dealer out of a store called The Tao of Wireless on Queen Anne. I was just going to run by there."

"I'll meet you."

The place was tucked between Dick's Burgers, where I stopped going when they started charging for mustard, and a Blockbuster that was feeling the pinch of Netflix. It was a one-man small-volume operation and the man might not have been a vegan, though his resemblance to an asparagus spear led me to believe that he was. Beckman presented his credentials and received the more-or-less expected display of willing cooperation.

"I'm interested in a phone you sold . . . last month, on the twenty-fifth, to a Baron Von Rothschild."

"Let me check my files."

"You get a lot of barons around here?"

"I remember the person; I just wanted to get the paperwork."

"Please."

"That's very recent, so . . . here it is."

He passed a sales sheet to Beckman, who gave it a glance.

"Yeah, I know all this. You said you remember the guy."

"Yes, and I'd be very surprised to learn he was really a baron."

"You think?" said I.

"Although he was definitely a German. He had an accent, not much of one, but clearly English was his second language. Besides, he *said* he was German."

"He did? Why?"

"Just explaining why he wanted a no-contract phone. He said he was a tourist and would only be here for a short time."

"Did he say where he was from?"

"Yes, I asked him. Munich. I said I heard it was beautiful there, and he said it was."

"What did he look like?"

"Nice-looking young man. Blond hair, in need of a haircut. Maybe six-foot tall and fit. In his twenties. Or maybe even his teens. Carried a shoulder bag. He came in with another kid, same age."

"Also German?"

"No, the other kid was from here. The German was using that kid's address."

"I don't think so. The address was a Starbucks in Bellevue."

"Hmmm. I thought it was a little unusual."

"What?"

"When he gave me the address, he read it off a book of matches."

Beckman and I looked at each other. He smiled, I don't know why. If I had any hair on the back of my neck it would have been standing. But that's me. Coincidences frighten me.

"Did either of them call the other by name?" I asked.

"Did they? Let me think. Besides the baron bit it was your basic no-contract phone sale. I want to say that one of them said a name. I just can't seem to remember."

"Was it Stefano?" I asked.

He took a moment.

"No, but I think it did end in O."

"Was it Bruno?"

"Yes! It was. Bruno, that's the name I heard."

"That's the man we're looking for," said Beckman.

"That was the other kid, not the German. Shorter, overweight, wore glasses. He advised the other on all the features of the different phones. A geek, maybe."

I leaned back on the counter, facing Beckman.

"Any ideas?" I asked him.

"Anything else you can remember?" he asked the phone man.

"Not really. As I said, just another sale."

"We think Bruno now has that phone," I said.

"I wouldn't be surprised. Often foreign tourists buy a pre-paid phone and then when they go home they give it to a friend to use up the remaining time, or they sell it. What has this Bruno done?"

Well, that was the problem, wasn't it? He hadn't done anything, except send threatening text messages to me, but with no threat to me, just to someone I don't know named Stefano.

Twelve

True downtowners call it 'Hellvue' and never ever go there. First of all, there is no easy way to get there, if there were any there there, which there isn't. You have a choice of two routes, both of which involve a bridge. You can go north or south to go east, but if you go south then you have to be part of Mercer Island for a while before going north again on the other side. It's probably not as complicated a decision if you're not me.

I drove the little PT Cruiser north to the floating bridge and over to the dreaded east side, where I found the Starbucks in question. I grilled the barista and two register girls about all things Germanic, especially about a good-looking German boy, the sort of customer these girls might remember while overlooking his chubby, geeky American friend with a blood lust for Stefano. I got nothing. To fortify myself for the drive back across the bridge, I ordered a single short and sat down. I put the earphones over my head and slipped another cassette into the recorder.

In the background, on the cassette, I could hear an odd whirring sound that I couldn't identify.

"If I did write my memoirs, I could use a bike trip as the frame for it. Maybe with the goal of seeing something in particular before it's all over, or to see something one more time. Or someone. I could make it a long ride and go back to the old school, back to Ithaca. I might draw a parallel with *The Iliad*, not that it hasn't been done before. Although Odyessus on a Harley-Davidson could be interesting, and I wouldn't mind seeing Cornell once again, cruise Collegetown on the hog, recapture old student days. No money, no girl, endless hours at the library, pre-pc's, pre-film schools, pre-communications majors. All that time spent sitting in Willard Straight over Camus and grilled cheese and bacon sandwiches, watching the snow fall, like, on an Easter Sunday."

"I don't have a clue to what you're talking about."

I was surprised to hear yet another woman's voice, this one with the hint of a lazy southern accent.

"Eunice, let the dude talk."

That voice I recognized as the rude man I talked to on the phone. They must have been at the tattoo parlor in North Beach. Then I heard the Devil Doll: "Yeah, you kind of got off the subject, though."

"Which was?"

"Tom Cruise."

"He was a nice young man. Called me 'sir.' Years later,when I went to see Timmy Hutton in Portland, where he was acting in one more forgettable movie, he told me that during the shoot he and Sean would go through elaborate ruses to ditch Tom on their day off because he always soured their action with the local girls. Who could have ever imagined that the socially awkward kid would be anointed the sexiest man in the world? Filthy rich? Choice of any role? Approval of director? Nicole Kidman? Penelope Cruz?"

I could hear the two lesbians giggle.

I turned off the player and read the words of wisdom on my Starbucks cup, life advice from a third-rate character actor on a cancelled sit-com. I tossed it and headed for the bridge.

Alex Krapp in a tattoo parlor in North Beach, San Francisco, telling behind-the-scenes stories to inkers and Devil Dolls? It didn't sound like the man I knew, and it didn't sound like he was enjoying himself. Maybe he was just trying out his idea of writing his memoirs and later came to realize there were better things to do. Like nothing. Like disappearing. With any luck, he might avoid my finding him.

I was on Route 5, heading south into the city. Just before the Stewart exit, traffic stopped. I called my office phone for messages. There was only one, left by a frightened voice: "Mrs. Quinn, this is Lars, from The Copper Gate. Listen, I got the shit beat out of me this morning and I don't know why. They said, 'Don't call the cops.' What the hell is going on here? I'm calling you because for sure I'm not calling any cops. I mean, that cop who came in, all he did was show me a picture and I didn't even know the person. Do you know anything about this? What am I supposed to do?"

He left a number so I called him back. He appreciated the call. I asked him to tell me what had happened.

"I came in to open the place and get ready for lunch, and outside the back door I got jumped by three guys. The one guy didn't touch me but the other two worked me over pretty good. They were skinheads, the two, and never said a word. Jeans rolled up at the bottoms, boots—they kicked me a few times when I was on the ground. The other guy was well dressed, and spooky. He just stood watching them and then said, 'Don't ever talk to cops.' That's all he said, and it was in a German accent."

"The well-dressed guy? What did he look like?"

"Tall. A dark overcoat and a hat kind of pulled over his eyes. That's all that registered. I mean, I was getting the shit beat out of me."

The description matched the German who paid too much for an advance copy of my book, who bought a cell phone with Bruno.

"What should I do, Mrs. Quinn? Should I called the police?"

"Doesn't sound like a good idea, Lars. The police probably won't find your skinheads, but the skinheads obviously know how to find you."

"Jeez . . . I think I'm gonna get out of town for a while."

"I'll see what I can do from my end, okay?"

"Thanks. Like what?"

"You never know; things come 'round in circles. That picture the cop showed you, you knew the guy was dead, right?"

"Yeah, I could see that. But I didn't know him."

"Maybe you did. Or maybe somebody thinks you did."

"I didn't! I mean, the guy was hardly recognizable to his mother."

"That's what I mean. You didn't recognize him but you might have known him."

"I guess it's possible. I work in a bar."

"Remember any German accents?"

"No, just once in a while a Mexican . . . or an old Swede . . . or a Russian . . . or like that guy who hung with Alex Krapp."

"Let's think about that for a minute, that guy with Alex Krapp. Can you remember anything at all, anything they talked about?"

"I never paid any attention. I mean, people talk about sports, about politics, about women . . ."

"Did they ever talk about women?"

"I don't know! I don't pay any attention!"

"All right, keep calm, it's not important."

"I remember once they asked for some wire."

"What?"

"Customers are always asking for something, a pen, a calculator, a dictionary. . . . I remember once they were sitting at the bar and one of them asked me if I had a piece of wire."

"What kind of wire?"

"Just the kind you have sitting around. Baling wire."

"You had some?"

"Yeah, in the junk drawer. A piece about eight inches long. I gave it to them. I figured they were working out some bar bet."

"What did they do with it?"

"I don't know. I went about my business."

"So they didn't give it back?"

"No."

"That's it?"

"That's it."

"Which one asked for the wire?"

"The foreign guy, I'm pretty sure."

I told him to take care of himself. I went home and parked the car and walked to Brasa for a martini, maybe two.

Thirteen

In the morning I felt trashed. I went to my office. It was trashed, too.

When I found the door open, I cursed myself for having forgotten to lock it the day before. Then I stepped inside and realized I'd been ripped off. My file drawers were crowbarred open and the contents strewn about the place. My desk drawers were tossed. Everything was pulled off the shelves. The strange thing was, nothing seemed to be missing. My laptop, which I had cabled to the leg of a worktable to make it a lot more difficult to take, was, well, untaken. The laptop was the most valuable thing in the one-room office. Second in line was the fifth of 101 Wild Turkey I kept around for medicinal purposes, and that still lay on the carpeted floor, unbroken from its fall.

I sat on my desk chair, put in a call to Beckman, and waited.

Most of the day before, I was out of the office. Anybody could have walked into the building and, experienced enough, unlocked my door. But no one knew where I was or when I might come back. The night entrance opened on a code pad, but in the past I've come in behind other tenants several times. No matter, breaking and entering in Seattle is on a par with car theft; in other words, only marginally criminal, unless drugs were involved. If my burglar was looking for drugs, he would have taken the laptop when he didn't find the genuine article and sold it cheap and quick. No, somebody was looking for something specific. It could have been some enemy of mine or of a past client, but the timing bothered me. Shelley seemed way too interested in those twenty cassettes, but I couldn't imagine her pulling this off, or why she would hire someone else to do it. The cassettes were useless. I thought about getting them back from Bernard, mailing them to her, and being rid of them. Then I thought better of it.

Sargeant Beckman showed up with another cop, who took some pictures, asked me some questions, took a cursory look at the doorlock, and disappeared. I didn't expect to hear from him again.

Beckman stayed behind.

"You're a detective . . . ," he began.

"A very good one, I've been told."

". . . heal thyself."

"Okay. Random break-in. Anything shows up, I'll call you."

"Don't be a wise-ass."

"I wouldn't have even called, but I wanted to see you, here, looking at this."

"Oh?"

"I talked to Lars last night. He's the kid who bartends at The Copper Gate. He got beat up yesterday. Unlike me, though, he's not calling any cops." I told him the Lars story. "Somehow," I said, "this has something to do with that."

"What?"

"I don't know, but it all comes with a German accent."

"The kid didn't know anything. He was of no help."

"Yeah, well, the Kraut and his thugs didn't know that."

"We got a hit on the John Doe, from Interpol and Immigration."

"God, don't tell me he's a German."

"He's not. He's a small-time Romanian smash-and-grab thief, here illegally. Name of Bogdan Mihailescu."

I should have known, and maybe at some level I did, because I wasn't all that surprised. It was like the sound of the other shoe dropping, only I was dealing with a three-legged man.

"Now I'm sure it all ties together somehow. The murder, my cell number on the victim, Bruno and Stefano, my being hired to find Alex . . . . "

"How so?"

"Alex Krapp used to hang out at The Copper Gate when he was in town. Lars remembers him talking to only one other guy there. A man in his mid-thirties with an Eastern European accent named Bogdan. Once they asked him for a piece of wire."

"What?"

"Forget about that. The point is, my Alex Krapp knew your Bogdan Mihailescu, who was murdered with my cell number on his body. I'll bet the farm Alex gave him that number. The Romanian wrote it down on a Copper Gate matchbook, using the European seven."

"Why?"

"Because he thought Bogdan might need my services. Then on the same day that the Romanian is dropped dead on Alaskan Way, I get a call from Alex's wife Shelley, who wants me to find her long-lost husband, whom she didn't live with and maybe didn't love enough."

"What's 'enough'?"

"Who knows? Now, it looks like she loves him all over again and thinks he's alive. She gives me a load of cassettes, cassettes that were with Alex on his ride, made during his ride, which argues for his being alive somewhere. I happened to mention that I had twenty other cassettes. She wants them badly, even though she's only listened to a few of the ones she gave me. All right, I don't know what that's about, but she tells me she's read an advance copy of ***Krapp's Last Cassette***, which she received from the publisher. I'm waiting to hear if that's true. I know they sent one to the Seattle Mystery Bookshop, though, and that one was bought by the same German who had Lars beat up. He paid fifty bucks for the book, a lot more than he had to. And Shelley paid me way too much."

"She's a rich woman."

"Yeah, and rich women don't want to pay for *anything*."

"This is true."

"And look, on the same day my cell number is found on a dead Romanian I get a text message, from someone with a German name, that Stefano has to die. What the hell?"

"Bruno, we know. He's a Seattle geek."

"But his friend is a German and sounds a lot like the one who bought my book and had Lars worked over."

"Why does the one thing have to have something to do with the other things?"

I was still stacking up the things.

"Okay, so why was my office broken into but nothing was stolen?"

"Shelley, this rich, classy, and beautiful woman of a certain age, was looking for those other cassettes, even though she had just given you a bunch of 'em," he said, as though it were an outlandish idea.

"That's what I'm thinking. Because there must be something of value on the ones I have."

"Like what?"

"Hell if I know. They're just recordings of his conversations with Danny, that boy, just random cassettes given to me out of a great bunch of conversations, so I'd have a sample of the voices of the principals. Just that and his last cassette, the one he gave me before he took off and disappeared."

"And what's on that one?"

"Not much. It was a very brief good-bye to me. A sense of sadness and loss, confusion, aimlessness."

"Maybe they were after something else in here, something you don't know about."

I started to pick up the stuff that littered the floor. "Alex has been missing for two years. Has Bogdan been carrying my number all that time? If he hasn't, then Alex gave him the number after he went missing."

"Or he didn't give it to him at all."

"Had to. Very few people have that number. And it's a solid connection. Alex and Bogdan hung out together. Come to think of it, why? Bodgan was a Romanian thief in his mid-thirties; Alex, an American screenwriter in his early-sixties. They had nothing in common."

"They liked to drink at the same bar. That's enough."

"Alex was always looking for movie ideas. Could it be this Romanian had a good story? If we knew the story, we might know everything, or at least have a better chance of putting it together. Oh, did we forget that the Romanian was murdered with a German Luger?"

Fourteen

A certain sadness fell over me as I headed south on Route 5 through a light rain. How quickly and easily I was able to leave town! No dog or cat to arrange for, neither budgie nor goldfish; no paper delivery to suspend or mail to hold; no need to give a key to a neighbor; not even any potted plants to be watered. On the other hand, why did it seem so difficult for me to leave town? A bag needed to be packed, cassettes to be sorted; the PT Cruiser needed to be fueled and oiled and inflated; a Bluetooth device needed to be synched and attached to the visor; a Magellan needed to be programmed for a crossroads in San Francisco; a Diet Coke needed to be put in the cup holder, and a bag of Fritos needed to be opened and put on my lap.

As always, I was uneasy to be so far beyond the city limits, heading into Olympia and building up my platform of paranoia.

For instance, a white van had followed me all the way from my alley in Pioneer Square and onto the interstate. When it passed me in Tacoma, I allowed myself a sigh of relief, but then I came upon it several miles down the road, moving so slowly that I was forced to pass it. It passed me once more, and just north of Olympia I passed it again. I told myself it was not uncommon on a road trip to pass the same vehicle several times on a long stretch of road. I tried to catch a look at the driver as I passed, but the rain made it impossible. I kept the van in my rearview mirror, with a nagging apprehension.

Midway between Olympia and the Columbia River, I pulled off into a rest stop and sat for a moment in the idling car. The van came in right behind me and parked on the opposite side, at the pet area. As soon as it stopped I wrote down its license number and backed out, then slowly rolled toward the freeway entrance, keeping the van in my mirror. Nobody got out of it.

I rolled onto the freeway again and kept my speed at sixty-five, listening to *Morning Edition*. Fans of a teenage vampire movie based on a series of vampire books were flocking to a little town not far from where I was currently sweating my tail. Forks, on the Olympic Pennisula. Forks? I'd been there. Apart from setting out to hook a steelhead trout, I could see no earthly reason to go to Forks. But, then, I guess the kids weren't going there for earthly reasons. For me, after three days in Forks, a vampire attack would be a welcomed way out. In the real world, the economy was continuing its downward spiral, sticking the new President with an unprecedented shit storm, and everyone was wishing that under that navy-blue suit he wore a cape and a big S on his chest. Hey, Californians elected a superhero as governor. In the real world, though, even Rambo could do no more when America was attacked by terrorists than man a phone in a fund drive for the families. I turned off the radio and scanned my mirrors. Inside of a few minutes I saw the van trailing behind me again.

Just before the bridge into Portland, I got a call from Shelley Lavendar. She sounded tired.

"How are you, Quinn?"

"Couldn't be better. How about you?"

"I'm devasted. I've lost my house, up in flames."

"I'm sorry. At least you're all right, ain't?"

"Yes, I'm fine."

"And the animals?"

"The dogs are okay. Frightened, but unharmed. We're all staying with friends. I've lost everything. Books, art, music, photo albums, a lifetime of memories. I know it could have been worse, but it was horrifying, walls of flame shooting up into the sky, the blast of a furnace on my face, me wondering if this was the end."

"It's good you gave me Alex's cassettes."

"What?"

"You have the cassettes, at least. Or I do, but I'll be returning them."

"And the others?"

"Those too."

"Do you have them now," she asked, and I could sense the urgency in her voice, the need.

"Not at the moment, but I have them."

"In your storage unit, still?"

"Yeah. Don't worry, they're safe. So what will you do now?"

"Do?"

"Your house and everything."

"Rebuild, I guess. But I'm not going to do anything until we find out what happened to Alex. It would be great to have some good news."

"Well, listening to the tapes, I'm more and more convinced that he staged a disappearance."

"I knew you would be! I was, too."

"He's been pulled in that direction for a long, long time."

"Yes."

"There's a good chance he'll make himself whole again and come back."

"We can't wait for that."

"We?"

Why did she say *we* and why did she take a beat? Of course, I was still hip-deep in my own paranoia.

"You and me," she said. "We have to find him. We're committed now."

"Oh, if he's alive, I'll find him. I heard him talk about disappearing thirty years ago, but he had too many responsibilities, he said."

"I wasn't one of them, not then."

"Whatever responsibilities he had this time, he didn't say. What he did say was he could maybe go cross-country to Ithaca."

"Ithaca?"

"Cornell. School days."

"Is that where you're going?"

"Who said I'm going anywhere?"

"Well, aren't you? Don't you have to?"

"Not unless I know for sure there's something to look for."

"How will you find out?"

"One thing leads to another. It always does."

"Where are you now?"

"In my car."

"I thought so. I hoped so. Where are you going?"

"On my way to Trader Joe's."

Which wasn't necessarily a lie. There was probably a Trader Joe's somewhere down the road.

"So you're in Seattle?"

"Where else would I be?" Still not a lie, just a question.

"Shouldn't you be on Alex's trail?"

"Who said I wasn't?"

"Well, are you?"

I had an unsettling feeling that she already knew where I was, that someone had told her, calling from the van that was tailing me.

"I thought I was going to have free rein."

"Of course. Naturally, I'm curious."

"I'll stay in touch."

I scanned the mirrors. The van was still tailing me. After I blew off Shelley, I called Beckman and told him where I was.

"You're sure you're being followed?" he asked. "You're not just being paranoid?"

"Yes, and maybe. Can you get to work on the license number?"

"Sure, I'm on it, but what are you going to do in the meantime? You could find a police station and pull in."

I had another idea.

I got off the interstate and took Route 14, following the signs to PDX, the airport. The van got off behind me and stayed with me. I pulled into the parking garage and my tail followed, removing all doubt that the van just happened to be going in my direction.

I pulled into a space and the van found a spot less than thirty yards away. I took the LadySmith out of my purse and locked it inside the glove compartment, since I wasn't licensed to carry a gun outside of Washington State. No parking garage in America is entirely safe for a woman to walk alone, but I didn't think I'd be any safer sitting there in my car. I grabbed my overnight bag and hurried to the skybridge, like any other passenger hurrying for a flight.

I went up to the Alaska Airlines desk and stood in line, occasionally turning to check behind me. I was one person away from the counter when I saw them: two skinheads, wearing parkas and jeans rolled up over high laced boots. They turned away as soon as I spotted them.

I bought a round-trip ticket to Seattle and put it on the Visa. Once through security I made my way to a customer-service desk where I exchanged my ticket for one to San Francisco.

Fifteen

I don't like San Francisco. I'd like to say it's cold and it's damp, and for that you can call me a tramp, but the truth is that I don't like any place that isn't Seattle, which is even colder and damper. Sometimes I'm not too crazy about that town either, but at least I know my way around, which counts for a lot in my head.

The BART carried me quickly from SFO to Union Square, and as subways go it wasn't bad. I came up in one piece.

On the plane, an Australian co-ed traveling on her own recommended I stay at the King George, a European-style (read small and cheap) boutique hotel. She, herself, would be staying with friends of friends, since she was on a severe budget. She'd been traveling for a year and had been just about everywhere and spent just about nothing. It's what Australian kids do.

I checked in, picked up a city map, and walked up Grant Street through Chinatown, where I bought a lotus seed moon cake for later. It was something of a hike to North Beach, but after the long drive and the short flight it felt good to use my props again. It was, I must admit, rather nice to walk in the sunshine. I don't get to do that much.

If you're going to live in San Francisco, North Beach is a better neighborhood than most. It reminded me a little of Pioneer Square or Belltown in Seattle. Everything was close, and people seemed to know just where to go. It was cocktail hour, depending on your watch, so I made a stop at Vesuvius, where legend has it that everyone who ever identified himself as a Beat Generation poet got tragically drunk during the late fifties. I ordered up an Anchor Steam, which hit the spot, so I had another. That made me practically a regular. The bartender had no trouble telling me where Slave to the Needle was, and I had no trouble finding it.

These days even spinster librarians have studs and tats in highly visible places, so my coming into the parlor raised nobody's eye brows. I noticed behind the counter a small Buddhist altar like the one I saw behind the counter of the Chinese bakery. I told them who I was and why I was there.

The tattoo artist was named Doc Roc. He was old school, a veteran of many summers of Burning Man. I'm not sure I would have trusted the steadiness of his hand. He wore an ugly gray beard and said nothing because, he explained briefly, he had nothing to say.

Boo was the name of the Devil Doll skin puncher, which made a kind of sense. She was a fright. A ring through each eyebrow, studded nose, a silver flight of steps up each ear, a ring from each end of the lower lip, rendering her mouth into a permanent unhappy face. She had frizzy black hair that was kind of cute. When she opened her mouth I saw a silver button on top of her tongue.

"A couple of years ago you took a motorcycle ride with a man named Alex Krapp," I said.

"Was that his name?" she said and giggled.

She wasn't cracking wise. She just never caught his name, and now hearing it struck her as funny.

"Yes. He was a screenwriter."

"We knew that. He told us stories about movies and stuff."

"*We?*"

"Eunice and me."

"Who's Eunice?"

"My wife."

I may have reacted, forgetting I was in California. Of course I was vaguely aware that same-sex marriages had been made legal in the state, and more aware that they had been somehow made illegal by the last election, a couple of weeks before. I could care less. You think marriage is a joy ride? Give it a shot. I would never deny anyone that experience. Or, as is my motto, put your face wherever it is welcomed.

"You know he went missing right after that," I told her.

"He did? No, I didn't know that. He's still missing?"

"That's why I'm here."

"Do they think anything . . . bad happened to him?"

"*They* do. They think he went off the road on US 1 and into the ocean."

"Shit."

"But I don't think so. Can you tell me anything about the time you spent with him?"

"He was a good rider, for an old guy. He was nice, a little tripped out but I was, too, when I met him. I had a bad log roll with Eunice and just bugged out of town on the bike, rode all night, and ran into him on the Redwood Highway. We ate a canteloupe together."

"Yeah, I know."

"How do you know? I thought . . ."

"He made a recording. He was always making a recording. I know you both rode together, south. What happened that maybe I don't know and ought to, if I'm to find him?"

"Well, we rode down to Bodega Bay. He wanted to spend the night there, and he said he would get a room for me. I went, why waste the bucks? We were practically in San Francisco. I went, let's push on and you can sleep on my sofa. So he splashed some water on his face and we got on 101 South. It's so cool to ride a bike across the Golden State Bridge and I could tell it lifted his spirits. We rode on to our place in the Western Addition. It was a little tense because I had to deal with Eunice, but he helped in that. He helped smooth things over. Next day he kind of wandered around the city."

"Did he say where? Did he mention meeting anybody?"

"I know he was in City Lights because he found a copy of a book he once adapted for a movie, that one with Tom Cruise. He said he thought about buying it because he'd never read it, but he didn't want to carry any extra weight. He took me and Eunice out to a nice dinner at La Colonial. After dinner I said I'd like to do something to repay him. He said we had, giving him a place to stay, but we really liked having him. I mean, my father would never stay with us. He thinks a bike is like putting a gun to your head. And Eunice's father, he never comes around either. Alex couldn't understand why, and I said, 'the hood, which is a little dangerous, the two of us, you know.' 'More's the pity,' he said. He was a cool old guy. So I said I'd like to give him a going-away present. I wanted to give him a piercing, free."

I chuckled, picturing his reaction.

"Yeah, he laughed, too, but then he noticed he hurt my feelings."

"Sorry," I said.

"That's okay. You don't know any better. He didn't know any better then. Piercing is an act of purification. And when I do it I connect with the body. It's pretty erotic, and I told him I'd pierced men older than him. I told him there was something freeing, something exhilirating and cleansing at the moment of penetration. Some people do it once and cherish it forever; others do it again and again. They have to, or else they forget."

"He didn't do it?" I couldn't believe that he would.

"He said, well, I guess I could do an earring. Was there a message, like right or left, gay or straight, he wanted to know. I asked him if he trusted me and he goes, 'You're twenty years old, how could I trust you?' Eunice is there and she goes, 'Boo is an old soul, a very old soul.' He goes, 'Okay, I'll trust your old soul. Right ear or left ear?' I go, 'Please, Alex, you show up with an earring now, you'd look like an insurance salesman. You need a piercing that can be a secret, all your own, since the rest of your life is so out there for anyone to see. A secret shared by you and those closest to you, who love you. Only one place to put that ring.'"

"Get out!"

"That's the place."

"He did not do that!"

"Oh, yes, he did. He knocked down three tequilla shooters and we all came here. He laid it out and . . . pop!"

"Okay," I said. "At least it's another means of identification. What happened then?"

"He stayed with us a couple more nights, to let it heal, took us out to dinner both those nights. He was very generous."

"Did he pay with a credit card?"

She thought about it and said, "No, he paid cash. He seemed to have a lot of cash."

"What did you talk about?"

"Movies, like I said, and funny stories. And we talked about, you know, what it's all about."

"What what's all about?"

"Life."

"Come to any conclusions?"

"It doesn't suck. It doesn't have to. You can make it better, for yourself and for others, a little bit here, a little bit there. He talked a lot about perception. Is what you see and hear real? What is real, if anything? I really liked talking with Alex. I hope he's okay."

"And then he just left?"

"Yeah."

"Did he say where he'd be heading?"

"Oh, yeah. Doc and him talked, too, and Doc used to ride back in the day, but he quit when Richard Farina crashed. Anyway, he told him he ought to take a ride to Zen Mountain."

"Where's Zen Mountain?"

"It's not really called that. It's Sonoma Mountain, up above the town of Sonoma, but there's a Zen center up there so everybody calls it Zen Mountain."

"And he went there?"

"I'm pretty sure he did. At least he said he was going to."

"Did he say where he was going after that?"

"I don't think he knew."

"And he didn't come back?"

"No, but we didn't expect him to."

Sixteen

In my rented Ford Focus I wound my way up the twisting road toward the apex of Zen Mountain. The night before, after leaving Boo and Doc Roc to their respective arts, I nibbled at my rich Chinese moon cake in my quaint little room and listened to one of the screenwriter's cassettes, made while he was tearing up this very mountain on an eight-hundred-pound Harley-Davidson.

"Buddhism is solid and rather appealing, as a code of life. But then, so is Christianity if you do it right, if you actually follow it, though it's required that you take the leap of faith, or no ticket to heaven. What I like about Buddhists is that they aren't preoccupied with death. Not even concerned. If you are here, they reason, then death is not; and if death is here, then you are not. What's to fear? I should slow down before I kill myself. But I don't want to be late either. Speeding like a madman to a Dharma talk is already a Buddhist contradiction. Wrong action, wrong thought. What about this for a movie idea: what book is read by every college freshman? ***Elements of Style***, by the dynamic duo, Strunk and White. Why hasn't anybody made a movie out of that? Build a movie around the sensuousness and passion of English, tying it all in with concepts of style. Not fucking fashion, *style*. We explore the question: what is style? Who's our lead? A writer. *Two* writers, a team like old Strunk and White themselves. What do they want? Elegance in life. Neatness. Simplicity. Grace, in an increasingly rude and loutish . . . possibly insane society. What's stopping them? A national pride in ignorance. A bold and shameless anti-intellectualism. In short, the dumbing down of America. Fuck! This is a terrible idea. Better idea: a legal comedy, period piece. Distant relatives of Hamlet sue for damages. Fuck! No good. You'd have to actually know about Hamlet. That's a small audience."

For some reason Krapp thought it necessary to record his negative reactions to his own ideas rather than pay attention to the road.

The sound of the crash was captured on the cassette, preceded by the screenwriter shouting out, "Oh, crap!" Or maybe he was crying out to his other self, like, Oh, Krapp, now you've done it! All I heard after the cry were thuds, crunches, soft impacts, brush being swept aside or under, and the engine falling silent, and Krapp falling the same way. Then nothing but the hum of the recorder itself, and later the call of a song bird.

Could he still be there? Dead and undiscovered in some remote ravine? But if he were, then who used his credit card to buy gas in Half Moon Bay several days later? And who would have sent Shelley this cassette I was now listening to?

I drove pass the entrance to the Zen center and found myself going down the other side of the mountain toward Santa Rosa. I turned off into a small vineyard and was able to back around and return to the entrance, where I pulled into a small gravel parking area. When I turned off the engine, I could hear roosters crowing. I saw some activity in the kitchen so I tapped on the screen door and asked a robed monk for whoever was in charge. I was told that, strictly speaking, no one was in charge. So I told him I was an investigator, and he nodded and said, in effect, that I had come to the right place, because they were all investigators, too.

"Take me, please, to the one you talk to," I said, "and if that's not possible, take me to the one *he* talks to."

He put a thumbnail under his front teeth and pondered.

"Follow me," he said, and led me up a short path to the entryway to their temple, where I sat on a bench and, as instructed, took off my shoes, while he continued to another level, where he disappeared behind a sliding door. In a moment he returned, bowed, placed his forefinger to his lips in a call for silence, though all I heard since I stepped inside were the roosters.

He led me to the sliding door, bowed again, and slid it open. I stepped inside and he slid the door shut behind me.

The Roshi was sitting on the floor, facing a larger-than-life-sized wooden carving of the Buddha. He was a bald man, sparkling clean in his robes, and was probably sixty though he appeared to be much younger.

I told him who I was and who I was working for and where I had come from, all of which seemed to fascinate him.

"A couple of years ago, a man was on his way here to a Dharma talk, maybe given by you yourself, sir. I believe he crashed his motorcycle nearby on one of those twisty turns. He must have had injuries and his bike must have been damaged. Shortly after, the man, whose name is Alex Krapp, went missing."

"Missing from what?" he said in a soft, soothing voice.

"Well, from everything."

"Can a part of everything be missing from the rest?"

"Happens all the time."

"Then the rest would cease to be everything."

Now, I have a soft spot for Buddhists. I agree, for example, that we live over and over and over and over and over until we get it right, if ever we do, but I really wasn't in the mood to get into any koanery with the Roshi.

"Let's say nobody I know has seen him in two years and I would dearly like to meet someone who has."

"We enjoyed our days with Alex Krapp."

"So you did know him, you spent time with him?"

"Yes. How can I help you?"

"By answering a few questions."

He smiled and said, "I will do my level best."

Seventeen

A zoned-in Zen Buddhist desires nothing more than awareness, to live fully in the moment. It was the lack of awareness that led to Alex Krapp's rear wheel going off the road on a hard left twist, spinning him around and high-siding him over the bike and into the bushes, the eight-hundred-pound Harley tumbling down after him. As he rolled down the ravine, mowing down tall grasses and short bushes, he could see and then not see and then see again the elephant gaining on him (symbolic, of course; the elephant is a powerful image in Buddhist lore), rolling in the same pattern and momentum as he himself. When it hit him, it was cantaloupe first (he had bought another one and bungied it to the back) hard against his visor, smashing it, both visor and cantaloupe. Krapp lay still and unconscious in the tall grasses, while the elephant came to rest an extra somersault farther down the hill.

A seminarian told me: "In walking meditation, I came upon a figure, a man who looked dead. He was face up, his arms spread out, very much in the corpse pose. I saw what I first thought was his head smashed into pulp. I might have gone into a momentary state of shock. Then I discovered that it was only a cantaloupe, all over his helmet, and I was so relieved I laughed out loud. Later, I was told he was a famous screenwriter. We get famous people up here, but we seldom know who they are or why they are famous."

Had an ambulance been called, Alex might have spent several hours in the emergency room and then been discharged, maybe the next day, but no one thought about calling an ambulance or anything else, though a call went through the trees and up the hill. Students of Zen came and gathered around his prone body and silently waited for him to regain consciousness or for them to lose their own. They acted as though they had been expecting him, as though people found their Zen center by many means and this one happened to be his, crashing a motorcycle. When he did come around, the screenwriter responded as all crashed motorcyclists do: "Am I still alive?"

Alex moved his neck and satisfied himself that it was not broken. He removed his helmet and saw for the first time the circle of red and gold robes around him and wondered if he might be making a scheduled appearance before some celestial court of appeals.

"We will be having a vegetarian lunch. You're invited to join us," said the seminarian who discovered him.

Krapp got to his knees and saw his Harley resting another twenty feet down the ravine. It didn't look too bad, considering. The windscreen was crushed and the saddlebags had popped and would need to be reattached. Probably the fenders as well. Cassettes lay scattered about.

"I have to gather my stuff," he told the Zen Buddhists.

"Your stuff has already gathered you," one replied.

He did have a little lunch with them, forcing himself to stay awake, though desperate to lie down and sleep. He remembered a concussion he suffered playing basketball and how he was kept from going to sleep, to avoid falling into a coma. So he waited for the tow truck and watched as two strapping young monks balanced the bike on the hillside as it was winched up to the road and put onto the flatbed truck that would take it to the Harley dealer in Petaluma. He could have gone down the mountain with the truck but he had to admit he was feeling puny. The monks tended to him and advised him to stay and rest.

"He said he would stay for just the night," the Roshi told me, "but I saw in him a gift to the temple, a gift containing equal parts of torment and joy, the best kind of gift."

That evening, at eight-ten exactly, the Roshi and the screenwriter walked together, so slowly that Alex wanted to shout. They found their way by the light of a full moon. Krapp told him of his journey, so far, omitting the irritating ring on his penis and several other details, concentrating instead on the quest, which was what? And would take him where? He did not know.

"I see," said the Roshi. "You choose to travel down strange roads, though you have a perfectly fine sitting place at home."

To Zen Buddhists all problems are addressed by sitting.

"I don't think I do," said Krapp. "I don't seem to be able to sit there . . . or anywhere. Just on my bike. That seems to be the only seat I have left."

"Maybe you can sit on that recorder you carry like a rice bowl." The Roshi had a good giggle.

"Does it bother you? Sorry. I forget things."

"Excellent. I work diligently to forget all things."

"I have a need for dialog. I mean, to collect it and store it."

"Conversations on the shelf, ten cents a line."

"You're making fun of me."

"You may make fun of me."

"I'm seriously seeking here."

"If you cannot find the answers where you are, where do you expect to find them?"

"Answers? I'm still trying to sort out the questions. My heart hurts."

"No one can avoid hurt. But anyone can avoid suffering."

Krapp awoke at four forty-five a.m. with the others, ten monks and several sesshin attendees, and he limped to the temple for morning sitting meditation, which he managed for eight minutes before his body cried out in pain. He got up from the mat and sat in a cane chair, the perch reserved for the infirm and undisciplined, where he lasted another ten minutes. Then he quietly slipped away to the kitchen, where he made himself a cup of tea. An hour later, life returned to the grounds, in slow motion. Krapp fell into step with the Roshi.

"Sorry about ditching morning meditation," he said. "I'm a hard case. Can't sit, can't walk. I'm a washout. I have insurmountable monkey mind. My internist thinks I may have become bipolar, but she's, like, just out of med school. Even now, I'm ahead of myself, wondering about breakfast. I'm starving."

"After we walk, and chant, each will make his own breakfast."

"Okay. I'm not a bad cook."

"We eat, if at all, very simply."

They walked in slow, silent steps and Krapp really did begin to feel a small sense of calm.

"Roshi, sir, do you think I can hang out here for a few days? I'll be happy to pay."

"The only way to stay is to participate."

"Of course, I'll be one of the guys."

"It is not easy."

"You ever try screenwriting?"

So Krapp joined in on the chanting, the cleaning, the working in the garden, the working in the kitchen, the walking, and, yes, the sitting, as best he could, given his monkey mind. Up in the morning at four forty-five, sitting meditation, walking meditation, sitting meditation, chanting, making breakfast, cleaning the temple, manual labor, a lunch of rice and tea, work, a dinner of rice and vegetables and tea, more meditation, more walking, and then a little bit more meditation before closing his eyes at nine and falling into a peaceful sleep. Krapp was as good as his word, bringing to the regimented life the hard discipline of an experienced writer. Still, sitting was a torture. He squirmed, changed positions, went from mat to chair and back again, fearing that at any moment they might kick him out, but no one seemed to notice the new monkey mind among them. The Roshi, if anything, was amused.

"I'm an utter failure," Alex told him during one of their walks. "I want to become a born-again Buddhist, really I do. I need to have a practice, but look at me, I can't even sit."

The Roshi whacked him with his bamboo stick.

"Hey! What the hell!"

The Roshi smiled and said, "Your chances for success are very great."

"They are?"

"Do you know why?"

"Not a clue."

"Because you are an utter failure."

"That's what I just said!"

"The successful man is always one wrong move away from failure. The failing man is always just one right move away from success. The one is fearful and benumbed; the other is hopeful and excited. Which one would you rather be?"

"I have a choice?"

The Roshi gave him another whack with his stick. "What is failure if not the brink of success?" he said. "Record *that*."

When he recovered from his second whack, Alex said, "Seen that way, we're all as close to success as to failure."

"As close to everything as to nothing."

"As close to happiness as to sorrow. I wish I had taken the time to be happier when I was young."

"The only happiness is to be dissolved into something greater than yourself."

"What would that be?"

"Anything."

Krapp took the Roshi's stick away from him and hit him with it. "Dissolve *that*," he said and handed the stick back.

The Roshi laughed from his belly and said, "If a thousand people call your name and you do not turn your head, then you can say you have achieved serenity."

"No thousand people ever called the name of a screenwriter. We are the anonymous in the field of writing."

"In itself quite an achievement."

"What should I do, Roshi?"

"When you are alone, you should behave as though you were in the presence of the King. Then, should you ever be in the presence of the King, you can behave as though you were alone."

The Roshi took him on as a project, but not even he, with his infinite patience and excellent backhand swing, could make the monkey sit still.

Even so, the holy man's enthusiasm held fast, though it took a practiced eye to see it. Like the Christian who demands accepting Jesus as the only way to salvation, the Zen master believes enlightenment can come only by sitting. But one can live like a Christian without ever accepting Christ as the Son of God. Likewise, a Buddhist can practice in any number of ways as he circles the cushion.

To be precise, there are forty-five thousand different ways to practice Buddhism.

"Serving tea?" suggested the Roshi as he walked with his slowest student. "Serving tea can be quite a demanding practice, yet possible for one unable to sit."

"I've been a coffee man since I was five. My old mom used to make me a hot cafe au lait against the upstate New York cold. I can't get over the notion that tea is somehow effeminate."

"Flower arranging? A most satisfying practice."

"Huh? Likewise, if I may say so. Where I come from, if you can't eat it you don't grow it. Any arrangement goes on the plate and then into your stomach."

"Sumi painting?"

"Would you believe I've tried it? And I failed. I kept sticking my brush into my mouth. I sometimes wonder if the ink was toxic and, you know, damaged my brain."

The Roshi took solace in the silences, taking slow and measured steps with coordinated breathing.

"I've often thought that riding a motorcycle is a meditation," Krapp mused.

The Roshi's head rose. Forty-five thousand and *one*!

"If you think about it, it has all the major ingredients. My feet and hands are in a fixed prescribed position. I find a loose focus on an indefinite spot somewhere straight ahead of me, down the road, looking neither right nor left yet taking in everything. The rumble of the engine . . . potato, potato, potato . . . keeps me in the moment and, sometimes, renders my mind a blank, so that I don't know how much time has passed."

"Is this safe?"

"Well, I'm quite aware of everything when I'm in the groove. Because I'm part of everything. What did the Buddhist say to the hot-dog vendor?"

"Make me one with everything," replied the Roshi flatly.

"I guess you've heard them all."

"I heard that one."

"Anyway, it doesn't work in a car. In a car you're listening to the radio, drinking coffee, on the phone; you're encapsulated, set apart from all the smells and wind and weather and just everything. Trapped. That's why bikers call them 'cages,' and the drivers 'cagers.' The problem is, and it's major, is that I sometimes get ahead of myself, planning, scheming, dreaming up scenarios."

"Do not clothe yourself before your birth."

"Right. That's why I ran off the road up here."

"We must find a practice for you, to keep you from running off the road again. Embracing truth, for example."

"That's a practice?"

"Oh, yes, a most demanding practice. One cannot lie under any circumstances."

"I work in Hollywood. I wouldn't know the truth if it jumped . . . down my throat."

Over the next few days several thousand other possibilities were raised and rejected as unworkable.

The monks gossiped about the tug of war between the Roshi and his inadvertent student, and they laid odds on who would crumble first. They saw it as epic comedy.

And then, on one of their long, slow walks, the Roshi said one word, "Gratitude."

"Gratitude?"

"Yes, a life of gratitude should be a given, but for some it is a respectable practice. To feel and express sincere gratitude for all that has happened, both the good and the bad. To be willing to do everything, to live every moment in your life over again. To be *grateful* to live every moment again, in exactly the same way."

"Including all that time with my first wife . . . and my second . . . not to mention my third?"

"Especially that. Every moment."

"Not working with Jon Peters, though. I wouldn't have to be grateful for that, would I?"

"I don't know who that person is, but, yes, everything. The only way to show gratitude for one thing is to show gratitude for all things."

"You strike a hard bargain. Catholics have it easy compared to you guys; all they have to do is confess."

"I believe the Four-Fold Path is much harder to follow than the Ten Commandments, but who's keeping score?"

"So you don't care much if I covet my neighbor's wife, which I've done once or twice?"

"Not at all. Covet away . . . but why?"

"Yeah, it is a waste of time."

"Be grateful for the time."

"I think I could live a life of gratitude, for both the good and the bad and the boring and the ugly."

"Think about it. Are you not grateful that you crashed your motorcycle?"

"Should I be?"

"Because of that you found this place and a time for rest. Karma."

"I'm grateful I didn't kill myself. I think."

"Are you not grateful that you have been given the life of a human being, against all odds?"

"Most days."

"Aren't you grateful that you have lived the life of a screenwriter?"

(There was a long pause on the cassette.)

"You know, I am. Sometimes I make it sound like it's the worst thing that can befall a guy, writing for the movies, but actually I'm very grateful I got to do it, especially during the seventies, when it was really exciting, when the execs let the filmmakers run wild, when the bottom line and the demographics didn't seem quite so important, back when you could make a studio picture for three mil and not have to apologize for anything. When you could make a movie about people and the things that they really do. Those were good times. And somehow I wound up rich. The thing you have to realize, Roshi, about screenwriting, what makes it what it is, is that in every other kind of writing the writer knows, deep down, if the work is any good. When a screenwriter submits his script, he's equally prepared to be told his work is *the best draft I've ever read*, or, *this is a piece of shit*. The game is to keep the screenwriter alive but in a constant state of impending humiliation. A delicate balance of praise and contempt is always in play. If you can handle all that, it's a good gig."

"Whatever it is, it will not always be so."

"From your lips to Buddha's ears."

"And whatever may happen may not happen."

"Now that I think about it, I can be grateful for all my marriages, as disastrous as they were. Excuse me, Roshi, but are you celibate?"

"I am. It is my choice."

"Then, excuse me again, but I'm also pretty grateful for all the women I've ever slept with, and *really* grateful for a few of them. Even now, adrift and alone, I should be grateful. Why not? I'm clean and sober, in pretty good shape, all things considered. My heart has a hole in it, but it's self-inflicted."

"Karma."

"I can't seem to trust anyone anymore."

"Trust yourself, and allow others to trust you."

It was a breakthrough. For his remaining time on Zen Mountain, Krapp practiced the fine and humbling art of gratitude, and with some success. His walks with the Roshi now bordered on quiet euphoria, and he gave serious thought to never coming down from that mountain, nor telling anyone that he was on it, but among the many things for which he was grateful, there was his motorcycle, not just the thing itself but the feeling it gave him while roaring to places unknown.

The Roshi listened with great fascination to Krapp's undeniable affection for his machine, a mere assemblage, after all, of gears and cams, rubber and cables, iron and leather, which Krapp had personified with the name Minnie.

"Let us give your motorcycle a new name, its real name," said the Roshi.

"Huh?"

"Let us call it your Dai-Jo We will make it official."

"What does that mean, and what would that do, exactly?"

"Dai-Jo," said the Roshi, "translates to 'The Great Raft.'"

"Raft?"

"Yes, The Great Raft is the metaphorical means of getting you across the wide and dangerous river. Everyone has one, whether he realizes it or not. For me, obviously, it is my sitting mat, and in this way Zen is no different than riding a motorcycle."

"So the Dai-Jo gets you cross the wide river. To what?"

"To the other side, what else?" The Roshi giggled. "There are sixty-two thousand kinds of rafts. Here on the mountain we prefer sitting or walking, koans, serving tea, floral arrangement, Tai Chi, drawing, chopping wood, and, yes, archery. You go a different way."

"If I go at all. Don't get me wrong, if there's another side, I'd like to get to it. I'd hop on the first Dai-Jo going that way."

"Ah, yes, but it has nothing to do with the raft, and everything to do with who steers the raft, because there is a sad and ironic danger inherent, in both motorcycle and Zen."

"I should have known."

"Most people become so attached to the Dai-Jô that upon finally reaching the other side of the river they are not able to give it up, are loath to push it away, and so, sadly, they are stuck there by the river's edge, one hand on the raft, forever."

Eighteen

Six days after Alex Krapp arrived at the Zen center in his un-Zen manner, he came back down the mountain, this time as a passenger in a Ford Escape. Contusions, of course, confusions, most certainly, but none of his bones were fractured and there had been little loss of blood. Nothing that a steady diet of rice and tea and meditation didn't cure.

He hitched a ride with a man named Porter, one of those men burdened with two last names. Porter was a Ford salesman, quite a successful one, in Petaluma. He owned a three-bedroom, three-bath house, had a semi-hot wife and a spunky pre-teen daughter. Life was good, and then his wife, upon reaching the age of forty, almost to the day, left him for a man ten years younger. Though still some distance from making an adequate social adjustment to his changing circumstances, Porter was at least functioning at an acceptable level, or had been, until he couldn't anymore and felt compelled to take a week off and go for on Zen retreat.

The screenwriter listened to Porter's story and fell into thinking about the terrible impact of multiples of ten upon the human psyche. One decade of life is gone, stacked and boxed and stowed away, and another one has been entered, closer to the swirling drain. Sixty was the worst. Or was it just the pinnacle at which everything pretty much goes fecal? As Krapp reflected on the passing of years, speaking into his recorder, all the way back to the minor trauma of leaving his teens behind him on his twentieth birthday, he could find nothing good happening on those pivotal dates. At fifty, seemingly out of thin air, he amassed bulk; at forty, divorced again; at thirty, his first kidney stone; at twenty an affair with a married woman who was thirty, mother of two, and wife of a favorite professor.

"None of these passages is obligatory," Krapp told Porter, "or even significant, if you have a solid practice of Zen."

"That's what they say."

"Pain is inevitable, yes, but suffering is not."

"You think?"

"Work on it."

Riding to Petaluma in the Ford SUV, Krapp was a little ashamed to see how quickly he could lose gratitude. Even reviewing the milestones was a form of lament, one of the things he wanted to be done with. Why not see the steps in a more grateful way? Independence at twenty, fatherhood at thirty, at forty the hottest writer in town and reasonably positioned to fuck women of all ages. At fifty, a multimillionaire, and no longer at risk of dying young. At sixty, free to jump on his motorcycle and go deep, with no mandate to return.

Porter asked the screenwriter, "Would you have written any movie that I might have seen?"

Questions like that make writers appreciate LA, where everyone just seems to know what you've written.

"Well now, Porter, you're asking me to be a psychic and I don't even have good intuition."

"Did you ever write for a movie star?"

"Yes, I've been fortunate."

"Like who?"

Krapp must have thought for a moment. There was a pause on the tape before he dropped a name recognized the world over.

Impressed, though he had not seen that particular movie, Porter asked, "Did she sing in that one?"

"Unfortunately, no."

"So how does it work, did she come to you with an idea and you whip it up into movie form?"

Another question that makes the cringing writer want to hurry back to LA, where everyone knows how these things work.

"It was a stage play first."

"Did you get to know her personally?"

"Of course. Once we worked for seven days straight in her home in LA. I took her out."

"Out? Like on a date?"

"Yeah, like on a date."

"Where did you take her?"

"To see a local production of the play I was adapting. It was arranged for us to enter the theatre just as the lights were dimming. We had two seats reserved in the last row. But we got there a few minutes early, so she took my arm and said, 'Let's take a little walk.' Her tone was almost childlike as though daring me. Her publicity agent and the limo driver kept us in view as we strolled the deserted Culver City street."

"Sounds romantic."

"Really?"

"Did you talk or just walk?"

I remember asking her, 'You don't get to do this much, do you, just take a walk down a street?' She answered, 'It would cause a riot.' She said it matter-of-factly, no irony or pride or self-pity. It was simply true. When we reached the corner we turned and walked back and slipped unnoticed into the theatre. The girl who played the lead was pretty good. It's a demanding role. Afterwards, we went to the Beverly Hills Grill and had cheeseburgers, fries, and beer."

"Cheeseburgers?"

"Movie stars eat cheeseburgers too."

"I'll rent that movie, now that I know you. When people rent one of your movies, do you get something, since you were the writer?"

"A little, and not when they rent it, only when they buy it."

"Buy it? Who would buy it?"

"I've often wondered myself."

"What was it like, working with somebody like that?"

"There *is* nobody like that. Those seven days I worked in her home were both excruciating and exhilarating. She was impossible, she was enchanting. I was miserable, I couldn't be happier.

We were making a last-ditch effort to save the project, which had already been knocking around for a long time. It was supposed to star Debra Winger, but Warner Brothers would much rather risk fifty million on her than five million on Winger, which really was the lesser risk, since the world markets would be sold before shooting ever started."

"Seven days. In her house."

"Long days. Nice house."

"What do you remember most?"

Another pause in the tape.

"I remember standing at a chalkboard she had wheeled into her dining room and writing three columns: Straight Fuck, Blow Job, and Hand Job."

"Wait, what?"

"For once and for all, we had to establish her rates, or the character's rates, because that was our problem, separating what a famous movie star could command from what a hooker who looked like her could reasonably charge. It wasn't easy, and because of the story we also had to establish how many of each she might perform per night, per week, per year."

"What did you come up with?"

And now, gentle reader, bear with me while I pull this episode together for posterity and film students everywhere:

• • •

"Let's say two hundred dollars for a straight fuck," proposed the screenwriter.

"Two hundred bucks! Are you nuts?" They both laughed, of course. "This is a high-class call girl, she gets a thousand, minimum."

"It's not for you, dear, it's for *her*. At a stretch, four hundred. Maybe five, tops."

"For a straight fuck? How much for a blow job?"

The diva and her collaborator stroked their chins.

"Men like blow jobs more than straight fucks," she said.

"I disagree," said Krapp. "One is only foreplay for the other."

"Christ, we forgot about half 'n half!"

Krapp added another column to the chalkboard.

"Let's just start at five hundred for a half 'n half and see where it gets us, okay? If the trick wants just a straight fuck, three hundred."

The movie star was not happy with the screenwriter chiseling down her rate on a straight fuck, but for the moment, as was her style, she allowed the writer to go on.

"A blow job," he continued, "is quicker. Time is money. So I would say two hundred for a blow job."

"How is it quicker?" she wanted to know.

"Less labor intensive . . ."

"*More* labor intensive! A straight fuck, all she just has to do is act; a blow job, she has to *work*."

"All right, but a blow job takes less prep time. You don't have to get undressed, cleanup is quicker . . . it's a pretty efficient sexual favor. Hell, you can do it in a car on your way to another trick."

"In a car! In a fucking *taxi*? She wouldn't do it in a car, for crissake, she's got class."

"I know, I know, I was just giving you a for-instance."

"Let's keep it specific to the character."

"If that's the case, I don't think she'd even offer hand jobs. It would be beneath her."

"Sure she would. Why not, if the john wanted one? Now, *that* she could do in a car."

"I thought you said she wouldn't do it in a car."

"She wouldn't go down on a trick, but—what the hell—she could jerk him off and make a phone call at the same time. Oh, I like that! Make a note to do a bit like that."

Krapp made the note and tucked it where he hoped it would not be found again.

"So," said the screenwriter, "what for a hand job? Fifty?"

"Make it a hundred."

"I wouldn't pay it."

"Yes you would."

Krapp wrote it down on the board, remembering that his father worked most of his life before earning a hundred dollars a week. "Okay, now the big question. How many tricks a night does she turn, and of what variety?"

Again, they each did silent computations.

"She's doing this out of defiance," she said. "One trick a night is enough."

"If she were doing it out of defiance, she might want to do as many as she could. She'd want to break the record."

"No, the personal satisfaction she gets out of this doesn't require more than one."

"Only one a night? No offense, but this is a . . . mature woman. She knows her marketability is going to drop soon, and soon after that, she's finished. She'd try to get as much as she could."

"It's not about the money. It's about control . . . and spite . . . and revenge."

"But she's getting older. That's a fact of life. How could she not be thinking about her nest egg?"

"Because she knows she's special and she will always be special. She doesn't hear any ticking clock. Men don't pay to be with her because of her beauty or her youth. She doesn't have either. They pay because she makes them feel so good."

She had a point. She made *Krapp* feel good.

"Okay," he said, won over. "One a day."

"And she would take two days a week off, to paint, to read, to study."

"Okay. That's five tricks a week. Let's say top of the line, five hundred a clatter. That's twenty-five hundred dollars a week. Does she take a week's vacation?"

"Two. She goes to Majorca, alone."

"Then at the end of the year she's earned . . ." Krapp did the calculations on the big board. ". . . she's earned a hundred and twenty-five thousand dollars. Tax free."

"That's all?" A moue of disappointment darkened the star's face.

"Sorry. You're just going to have to turn more tricks," said Krapp, like a hard-nosed business manager who's down for five percent of a slow client's income.

Then the tape went dead.

Nineteen

For dinner, I had a double-double with fries and a diet Coke at the Petaluma In-'N-Out, a little bonus of finding myself in California. There I got directions to the local Ford dealer. I hoped the place was still in business. I hoped Porter was still working there.

I pulled to a stop under the spooky cold glare of car-lot lights. I had only one foot out of the car before a young Mexican was all over me for a test drive in something, anything. I told him I was looking for the salesman named Porter. He got on his walkie-talkie and said begrudgingly, "Porter, customer waiting, customer waiting for Porter." The Mexican kid slunk away, and Porter came trotting out of the showroom toward me, wishing me well and good evening and how could he help me. I wiped the glow off his face by confessing that the Ford I was in was a rental and I wasn't in the market for a new car. I mentioned Alex Krapp's name. He brightened.

He invited me inside and we sat at a negotiating table. Hovering around the edges of the showroom were car salesmen nervously watching us out of the corners of their eyes.

"It's nice to hear his name again. Now, how do you know him?"

I gave him my card.

"Seattle?"

"Alex was a client once."

"I thought he lived in L.A."

"He had a place up there, too. Divided his time between the two places. Until he took off on his Harley and disappeared. That was two years ago, right after he came down the mountain with you."

"What do you mean, disappeared?"

"Like no one's seen him since, disappeared."

"Damn," he said softly. "Two years ago . . . that can't be good."

"His wife is hopeful. So am I, but one way or another we'd like to know what happened."

"I liked Alex, the short time I knew him, but I don't know how I can help you."

"I listened to his cassette, the one he made riding down with you."

"Yeah, I was taking him to the Harley dealer. They were fixing up his bike there. All the way down he had that recorder going."

"Not all the way. At a certain point it stopped."

"Yeah, he was telling me this story, and then he said, 'Porter, why the hell am I doing this?' It was like a turning point in his life. He said he was done with recording everything."

"What did he say after that?"

"He popped the cassette out of the recorder —and he threw the recorder out the window."

"So how did I get the cassette?"

"I don't know, except he asked me to stop at a mail-box place. He said he needed to buy a box and ship out all his cassettes, all that were with him and still on his bike."

"Ship out where?"

Porter tried to remember. "He was filling out the form in the car, while we rode to the Harley dealer. Who was it?"

"Was it to himself?"

"No, it was like he wanted to get rid of them, but he couldn't bring himself to throw them away, not like he did the recorder."

"Was it to his wife Shelley?"

"Never mentioned his wife. I remember! Gwendolyn."

"His secretary."

"Right, he said it was his secretary, in LA."

"Did he say where he was going, after he picked up the bike and got rid of the cassettes?"

"Yeah . . . south."

"Where? Santa Barbara? LA? Half Moon Bay?"

"I remember he said he needed more time to process the Zen experience. The time on the mountain was good, a good start, but he still had a lot to think about, decisions to make. I told him about Big Sur, how it was a great place for that."

"Did he say he would stop at Big Sur?"

"He said he thought it was a good idea; he could find some little place there to sit and stare at the moon."

Nothing was inconsistent with the police conclusions: he went off the road somewhere along Big Sur and went into the Pacific. Except if he did find a place to sit and stare at the moon, in the wilds of Big Sur, he might still be there.

I got a motel recommendation from Porter and tried to reassure him that Ford was not going to go under, not in America. Then he tried to reassure me.

Twenty

Inching along with the commuter traffic on 101 south, I finally crossed the Golden Gate Bridge in a foreboding fog and kept going south, through Pacifica, where the trees have been trained to one side by the coastal winds, and into Half Moon Bay. I stopped at the same Chevron station Alex had, one of those big places that sell gas, food, and almost everything else, the last place he used his credit card. No one there remembered him because none of the employees had been there two years before.

I burned through some minutes on my cell phone, first trying to get the number for Twentieth-Century Fox and then weaving my way down through that corporate structure to the lowly secretarial pool and finally to, "Spike McGee's office."

"Gwendolyn?"

"Yes?"

"This is Quinn."

"I'm sorry?"

"Couple years ago . . . spent a day there with your boss Alex?"

"Quinn! Of course, how are you?"

"Who's Spike McGee?"

Her voice dropped to a whisper. "The next big thing. Writes graphic novels. Draws them really, there's not much writing in them, but the studio is very keen on him."

"Same office?"

Still whispering, "No, it's a cramped little dump but he seems to enjoy it."

"And you?"

"Just counting the days. But what's going on with you?"

I had no reason not to tell her. On the other hand, I had no need to tell her too much. "Well, I find myself wondering again about your old boss."

"God, who doesn't? So sad. I sure miss working for Alex. I never had it so good."

"Before he disappeared, just before, did he ever get in touch with you?"

"No. He used to call daily, when he wasn't going to be in the office, just to see if anything was up, but one day . . . the calls stopped."

"No letters or packages."

"No. Oh, wait, there was a package. A bunch of his cassettes. Then nothing. And no one ever heard from him again."

"No note with them?"

"No, nothing. At the time I didn't think much about it. I just put the cassettes with all the others."

"Where are they now?"

"Oh, I sent them all to Shelley, his wife, after they recycled his office. I didn't know what else to do with them."

"When they closed the office? That was just a few months after he disappeared, right?"

"Right."

"So you didn't send her anything recently, like in the last couple of weeks?"

"Lord, no. I never had much contact with her anyway. Sending her his stuff was the last I ever had to do with her."

South of Half Moon Bay the fog lifted and I had a sunny pleasant drive down US 1. I saw a few spots where a bike might have gone into the deep blue, or the foggy bottom, or an inaccessible ravine, but after that, on in to Monterey, it seemed unlikely that he would have gone off the road witout being discovered by someone. Then I saw a highway sign warning of seventy-eight miles of twisty road. Along that seventy-eight miles were a lot of places to go off the map and into oblivion. Oddly enough, I found the drive relaxing, or maybe it was just the harmonic convergence of legendary Big Sur, which, since it isn't a defined piece of real estate, might really be a state of mind. I wasn't sure just when I entered it, though I knew I had, and I wasn't sure when I might exit it, though I thought I was getting close.

I pulled off the road at Nepenthe's, Big Sur's famous watering hole. It was warm enough to sit outside, so I sat at a long wooden counter facing a spectacular view of the coastline. A waitress came and I ordered a cheeseburger with fries and an Anchor Steam. I wanted to put a call into Beckman, but was so into the mellow vibe that I couldn't bring myself to contact that other world. My beer arrived. I had a swallow and took out my phone, but still didn't press Beckman's button. Before I knew it my burger and fries arrived. I didn't realize how hungry I was, or that I was having for lunch the same thing I had for dinner the night before, except this cheeseburger cost seventeen dollars. The view made it worth it. The night before, in Petaluma, I was looking at a freeway off-ramp.

The waitress was friendly and lingered to chat. Maybe she was curious about a woman my age traveling around there alone. It was November and most of the tourists had come and gone.

"Would you believe I'm a detective?" I told her.

"No way."

"What did you think?"

"Empty-nester, recently divorced, bailing out, like that."

"You're close on the first two counts. The divorce isn't all that recent. But I'm not bailing out of anything. I'm supposed to be working. I don't know, up here that feels wrong. No offense."

She laughed. "You think I'm working?"

"I'm looking for a man."

"Honestly, around here you don't have to look, except inward."

"I never mastered the knack. No, the man I'm looking for came here, maybe, around two years ago. He was on a Harley and he was looking for a haven, a place to just hang out, pull himself together. He had no contacts, as far as I know. Just a guy rolling into town, or whatever. Where would he go?"

"Maybe here. He'd have a beer and a burger and ask me where he could spend the night."

"And what would you tell him?"

"I'd say, go down the road ten miles to Esalen. See if they have a room. Soak in the waters. Do a little yoga, a little ecstatic dancing. Get a massage. See if anything comes to you."

"Sounds like a plan."

"It's a good start."

"Ten miles?"

"On the right. Be careful. You can miss it."

I finished my lunch and thought I'd have another beer. Then I thought better of it. Finally, I was ready to call Beckman.

"Where are you?" he asked.

"Could be heaven."

"And they're okay with that, you being there?"

"Don't be a wise-ass. What have you got for me?"

"The van that you think was following you . . ."

"Oh, it *was* following me."

". . . is a long-term rental. The customer is named Ulmann Maier, a German tourist."

"Germans again."

"You're breaking up a little. Can you hear me?"

"Yeah. Reception's probably spotty way the hell out here. Could this be the same German tourist who bought a phone and gave it to Bruno?"

"Lots of German tourists come through."

"They do? Why?"

He thought about it. "To have a latte at the first Starbucks."

"By the way, I haven't heard from Bruno lately."

"Well, no dead dudes named Stefano have turned up, so . . . ."

"So what are you going to do about the van?"

"Nothing."

"Nice talking to you, flatfoot. If some skinheads don't kill me maybe we can have a drink some time."

"If I don't kill you myself."

"I wouldn't want to inconvenience you."

Twenty-one

The waitress was right. By the time I saw the Esalen sign I was already past it. I had to drive another few miles to find a place wide enough to turn around. I turned into the driveway and down a steep incline, where I was stopped by a staffer in a little guard house. She was young and attractive enough except for the wispy moustache. I had to find my emergency brake because the hill was so steep. The girl wanted to know if I was registered for a seminar. I told her I just wanted a room for the night. She called the office. I was in luck. A room was available.

I parked the car in a line of others on a macadam and gravel roadway alongside a row of funky cabins built against a hill. On my way to the office, across an expanse of lawn, I saw a small swimming pool and several naked swimmers in and out of it. Someone on the deck was practicing Tai Chi.

Over the counter in the office, as the girl ran my credit card, I eased into some small talk. Most guests, she told me, come for a weekend or a week and participate in a wide array of new-age seminars, anything from Getting Unblocked: Opening to Silence to Cortical Field Reeducation and the Feldenkreis Method. If space is available you can stay and do nothing, enjoying the hot springs and the meals made from their own organic gardens.

The odds were slim that Alex might have stopped here, and if he did, would anyone who might remember him still be hanging around? They had extended work-study programs but rarely did anyone stay more than six months. Some paid staffers and seminar leaders lived on the grounds and were there for longer than the past two years. I might get lucky with one of them. Otherwise it looked like a pleasant way to spend a night.

I got my key and unloaded my overnight bag and carried it to one of the cabins on the hill above. It was what you might expect: paper-thin walls, scratchy towels, those flaky little bars of white soap, dim lights. Sheets were provided, along with a comforter and a prison-style blanket. I had to make the bed myself. I was fine with all of that, but no one told me I'd have a roommate. I'd have to interact on a social level. Her stuff was in the closet and laid out orderly on her pine dresser, along with a still-burning stick of incense. I was putting a few things away when she came through the door.

"Oh, hi! Gee, at last! I've been hoping for a roommate, but for the past four days . . ."

"I'm only here for the night."

"Drat! Well, I'm Bebe."

"Quinn."

Bebe looked harmless. She was from Sante Fe, on the far side of forty, dreading the loss, I imagined, of her physical beauty, of which she was given more than a fair share. I could have offered her one good beauty tip she hadn't thought of: stay out of the brutal New Mexico sun. Fostering now her inner beauty, she was. Taking a week-long course in reading auras, she was.

"I could read yours if you've got a few minutes."

"Maybe later."

"It's easy, really."

"What else do you do? Besides the aura-reading thing."

"I have a little shop in Sante Fe. I make bird houses."

"Last year even birds could have got mortgages, ain't?"

She laughed and looked like she was going to give me a little slap on the arm, which she wisely turned into an "oh, you!" wave.

"You talk funny," she observed.

"I do?"

"My bird houses are art pieces, but fully functional, too. Each one unique. I have a portfolio, if you'd like to see what I do."

"Let's do that. Sometime."

I made the act of putting away my few things appear a matter of serious concern.

"And you're just here on a personal retreat?" she asked me.

"More or less." Retreat forward.

"One night is hardly enough. I mean, this is a sacred spot. It takes time to get in harmony."

"I'll play it by ear."

"I hope you stay longer. I'd like to get to know you better."

I was a bit rueful that I had stopped in the first place, but I would, as always, make the most of it.

She dropped her jeans and stepped out of them, at the same time pulling her T-shirt over her head. She wore no underwear, so I was already getting to know her better than I wanted to. Her bikini lines were as wide as shoe strings. Except for her over-exposure to the sun, she kept damn good care of herself. She pulled on a pair of sweats.

"I'm going down for a soak. Would you like to join me?"

"I didn't bring a bathing suit."

She laughed. "Silly! No one wears a swim suit to the baths. C'mon, girl, I'll show you the way."

I let her lead me down the hill to the baths, which are cut into the side of the cliff, overlooking the vast and beautiful Pacific Ocean.

The deal was, you had to go through this cinder-block building full of showers and stacks of towels. The pools were on either side of the showers. One wing was marked "Silent;" the other, "Quiet." The showers were communal. I found myself showering between a man who was hairy everywhere but on his head and my new friend and roommate Bebe, next to whom I really didn't want to stand naked either, comparatively speaking. Though the hairy guy made me look good, she made me look like a hairy guy. He was a software programmer from San Jose, recently known to Bebe. They chatted about energy and balance, about the need to integrate mind, feelings, body, and soul into a unifying principle, a conversation to which I had nothing to add. Finally, Bebe escorted me out to the baths themselves, to the "Quiet" side. I had the feeling the programmer was right behind me, checking out my ass, something I don't even like people I know to do, though to be honest, I was checking out Bebe's, out of envy, of course. In short, I was uncomfortable and a tad overwrought by the time I paraded past two concrete pools and four ceramic tubs to the first of two stone pools. Bebe stepped inside and I went in after her. A scattering of naked bodies soaked or sunned or strolled around me. It took a minute to adjust to the hot water. I wondered when the memo went out that all women over forty must eliminate pubic hair completely or at least to a narrow landing strip and why I never received it. I sat down and in a few minutes all of that cultural stuff was out of my head.

I imagined Alex finding this place, relaxing in one of these stone pools after pounding the road on his Harley, finding some escape from all that had happened. I'd probably be able to talk the girl at the desk into checking the records during the time he might have been there, but I already knew that he didn't use a credit card, which meant he probably didn't use his real name either. It may have been here, on this beautiful cliff, that he made the decision to disappear, which to my thinking set into motion *something*, something that was culminating in violence and murder a thousand miles away.

There were six of us in the pool now. It was getting crowded: Bebe, the programmer, me, two more women (hairless down there), and a gray-haired, stooped old man I tried not to look at.

After everyone else said where they were from and why they had come, they wanted to know about me.

"I'm from Seattle," I said.

So there was some whispered small talk about that, the rain and all, and then I said, "I'm here actually looking for my brother."

All of them were on spiritual quests, so the concrete nature of mine caught their interest.

"Two years ago he disappeared somewhere around here. He was on a motorcycle trip. Everyone thought he drove off the road and fell down into the ocean."

Sighs of sympathy.

From where I sat I could look down the coast. The two narrow lanes of Route 1 were so high and so close to the edge. As easily as

I pictured Alex soaking in my pool, I could now picture him hurling through the air and down into the deep blue Pacific.

"But I don't think so," I went on. "I think he had some kind of mental breakdown. It's possible he stopped here for a while. I was hoping someone might remember him. Our other brother just died and I can't believe he wouldn't want to know about it."

I felt a little guilty being the center of all their effusive sympathy. On the other hand, it worked. They promised to ask around for me.

The old man and the programmer left. A young man and two women my age replaced them. Damned if the two older ladies weren't shaved as well. I was feeling conspicuous. Finally, the healing waters sucked away my bad *chi*. I hauled myself out, showered, and put my clothes back on. I walked the path back up to the center of the place, the dining hall, and had a cup of chai. Then I went back to the cabin for a long restful nap. Slept like the dead.

Twenty-two

Nothing bores me more than listening to someone describe a dream, so it's enough to say I had a dream about Alex, and not the first time, an ambivalent dream that I wasn't ready to wake out of, but Bebe, my new roommate, still naked, gently shook my shoulder and told me I shouldn't miss dinner, which was being served.

She got back into her jeans and T-shirt and put on a fleece jacket because the nights there were cold. I splashed some water on my face, and together Bebe and I walked to the dining hall and got into line. We loaded up on Polenta Napoleon—I figured the zucchini on top made it Napoleonic—and Swiss chard. We made a trip to the salad bar and had some "local 'chokes with chili butter" and some Esalen-grown greens. To drink: fennel tea.

"Oh, I have some news for you." Bebe said. "I almost forgot. That old man who was with us in the pool? He talked to someone who lives here, who said he remembers a man on a Harley around that time, two years ago."

My heart raced. If Alex had been at Esalen, it would be the only sighting south of Half Moon Bay.

"Who is this guy? Where is he?"

"He's a protégé of George Leonard, teaches akido and Gestalt therapy. I don't know his name. I don't even know him to see him, but the old gentleman would."

She looked down the line behind us and at the small scattering of people already sitting at the long communal tables.

"He's not here yet, but everybody comes to dinner. We'll see him."

We finished and went for dessert, Johnny's Vegan Wacky Cake. Against all my expectations, it was delicious. We had a second cup of tea and I grew anxious that the contact would skip dinner. Bebe put her finger to my forehead.

"It's what we're supposed to do when we see somebody getting lost in their own head," she said.

"Yeah, thanks. Won't happen again. Where the hell is this old man?"

A man wearing a serape and looking wind blown suddenly loomed over me. He held a plate in each hand and bent forward. He said in a soft voice, "Excuse me, are you the one inquiring after a man on a motorcycle?"

I almost jumped off the bench. "Yes, yes, that's me."

"May I join you?"

"Please, yes, sit down."

I slid over, putting enough distance between me and Bebe for him to squeeze in. He took his sweet time.

"It's your brother, I understand."

"Yes, and the rest of the family is sick about it."

He slowly sampled the polenta, then said, without looking at me, "What would you say to him?"

Huh? What business was it of his, the meddling jerk? But I was cool.

"Oh, I would say so much, but first that I love him and respect his decisions. I would tell him how grateful I was to find him alive."

"No, I mean, if he were sitting here. Pretend I'm him."

Normally, I wouldn't get pushed around like this, but I sucked it up and said, "I love you and respect your choices. I'm so grateful to find you alive."

He nodded in a gesture of approval.

I was glad that was over.

"What would you say to his motorcycle?"

Da frick, I wanted to smash his head with my coffee mug.

Bebe, who knew this territory far better than I, since I knew nothing and she had four hours of auditing a Gestalt workshop, jumped in and said, "Oh, can I be the motorcycle? Ask me, ask me."

The seraped yonko smiled and urged us to have a dialog. Once more, I'd have to go along with the gag.

"Okay." I struggled for something to say, and then I remembered the cassettes that Alex recorded up on Zen Mountain. "You were his meditation cushion."

"I was his meditation cushion," Bebe intoned gravely.

I did a nonplus and stared at her. Yeah, I just heard that somewhere.

"When he was straddled over you he was able to forget about all the uncertainties and disappointments and his sense of not belonging anywhere. Humping hard down the road put everything else out of his head."

Bebe seemed about to break a sweat with the sexual imagery.

"Yes, when he was riding me hard, his head was totally clear." She sighed, and appeared to look for a cigarette.

"Okay, now, thanks for the exercise but I'm desperate to find my brother," I said to the akido teacher, who was rearranging his Swiss chard. "Please, I really need to know, what do you remember about him, anything?

"Well, is your brother named Danny?"

"Oh, that's not a good sign."

"Do you think it was a different man?"

"No, it's his choice of an alias. It's a long story. Tell me more of what you remember."

"He came here on a big black Harley-Davidson motorcycle. He was six-foot tall, maybe six-one, and he weighed about two hundred pounds."

My heart raced again. It was him. It had to have been Alex.

"He wasn't registered for anything, but when he found there was a place available in my Gestalt group, which was a week-long session, he signed up for that."

"Did he talk about anything?"

"Oh, yes, but reluctantly. I can't remember really much of what he said. So much is said by so many during the course of the week, but I do remember he did not want to take the hot seat, which surprised me. Most of the participants can't wait to get on it, that's why they came, but he held back. He listened to the others, sometimes taking notes, which is also unusual. No one takes notes. I mean, how can you while reaching for catharsis?"

"He didn't use a recorder, did he?"

"No, we don't allow that." No. He wouldn't have anyway, because he tossed his recorder on the way to Petaluma. "When he finally did have to take the hot seat, on the last day, he recited a poem from memory and broke down sobbing. But then, everybody sobs over something. That's the whole idea."

"What was the poem?"

"Oh, that thing by Hugh Mearns. *'Yesterday upon the stair/ I met a man who wasn't there./ He wasn't there again today/ I wish that man would go away.'"*

I didn't say anything for a long moment. Anyone else, the poem might evoke a smile, but Alex had been thrust unwittingly into a twisted reality. I had to fight back my own tears.

"Other than that, I really don't remember much of what was said. I've probably revealed too much already."

"No, it's fine. When he left, did he say where he was going, or anything?"

"He left with a woman."

"He did? Someone he met here?"

Why was I not surprised?

"Yes, a local girl. After one a.m. the baths are open to the locals. I'm sure somebody knows her name. Anyway, I noticed that your brother and this girl were kind of hooking up. It happens."

"Yeah, sure, what doesn't?"

"I hope I've been helpful."

"You have no idea. What does this girl look like, the local girl?"

"Late thirties, early forties. Shoulder length auburn hair. Athletic body, no tattoos, warm smile. She's here almost every night, stays for about an hour."

I had time to kill.

Out of gratitude, I let Bebe take me to her evening session, held at Huxley Hall, where I offered up my aura, like an artist's model, posing before the group. It was the least I could do. A dozen or more participants circled round me, jockeying for a good vantage point, and then, one by one, they rendered their interpretation of what they saw surrounding my head.

Violet, said one; orange, said another; reddish-brown said a third. The leader, an awkwardly moving horsey lady from Montreal, complimented them in a barely audible voice on their powers of observation and prodded them to go deeper. Comforting, suggested one. A little frightening, ventured another. Strong, felt another. Nobody said: Liable to self-combust at any moment. Quick on the trigger. Tongue-tied. Lonely, loveless, and in denial. Hell, I settled for strong, comforting, and a little frightening, and figured myself ahead of the game.

After the session I found a weathered Adirondack chair near the edge of the rolling lawn, high above the water, so far beneath the twinkling stars. I wanted a martini to go with all of that. I'd discovered too late that they had a tiny bar that served beer and wine for about twenty minutes before dinner, then shuttered up, as a concession to the rich people who came in and were used to wine with dinner and as a compromise to the others who considered alcohol a poison and had difficulty standing by while others ingested it. I sat down in the chilly night air, stared up at the western sky, and thought about this new woman; 'girl,' he called her. Was she a 'campmance,' intense but over in a week? Or is he with her still? If he is with her, why doesn't he come back to the baths, like one of the locals? He's not with her, I thought. I hoped he wasn't with her, but more than that I hoped she would come tonight and tell me something that would make sense. He has a wife, that much is still true, though he has rejected her completely, if he is still alive. If he is still alive, he has rejected everything. Or replaced everything with something else. Two years later and Shelley is desperate to find him, because suddenly she believes he is alive, because someone delivered the cassettes he had with him. Those same cassettes, however, were sent long before, by Gwendolyn, his secretary. So Shelley is lying, at least about that. Why? Money, power, love? What is Shelley after? What am I after? I do this for a fee. It's simple, I kept telling myself, but nothing in the last week has been simple. Shelley wants me to find Alex, who used to hang out at The

Copper Gate, where he had a friend with an Eastern European accent. A Romanian is found dead on the street with my cell phone number in his pocket. Skinheads beat up a bartender for talking to me, and then follow me to Portland. A German pays too much for an advance copy of my book about Alex. Another German, or the same one, buys a phone and gives it to Bruno, a young geek, who texts me that Stefano, whoever he is, has to die. Again. Simple it isn't, and that's before we get into my own feelings about Alex, which I've already done enough of and don't want to do anymore.

I saw a shooting star.

Twenty-three

Late that night I got to the baths, showered, and wrapped a towel around my middle. The baths were more crowded than I expected them to be at this late hour. Everyone checked out the new girl. Fortunately, the light of the moon was kind. I took off my towel, hung it on a nail, and slipped into a pool with four or five others, who by that time had turned their heads and either resumed their whispered conversations or sat in silence staring at the stars.

By one o'clock in the morning I was the only one remaining in the pool, and frequently I had to sit on the edge to keep from dissolving. Only one of the pools was occupied: a man and two women, their heads back and eyes closed. I heard some hushed conversation coming from the showers. In a few minutes that all settled down when a line of ten to twelve people, the locals, silently walked outside toward me and fanned out, moving toward different pools. I could hear their sighs as they lowered themselves into the hot mineral water. Two young men with flaxen hair of gold and copper and lean firm bodies eased into my pool, nodding hello. As casually as I could, and by this time accustomed to my own public nakedness, I scoped out the other pools, looking for the girl to match the Gestaltist's description. I couldn't find anything close. Would I have to spend another day and night? Sharing the energy of the two Adonises in my pool made that a less-than-odious option.

Then she appeared.

If the moonlight is a friend of middle-aged women like me, it is a fan of women like her. Her skin was the color of cinammon, carmelizing in the Pacific moonlight. She carried no towel, only herself, with poise and confidence. Her stomach was flat, her breasts small and upright, her auburn hair all around her shoulders and below a dark rich triangle of fur. Bravo for that. God, she was young.

Her eyes seemed to be on the outermost pool, but before she could walk by, one of the boys whispered, "Hey, Maria. Soak with us."

She cast another glance at the far pool, as though looking for someone and not finding him. Then she stepped down into my pool, whispering a soft, "Hi, everybody."

For a few moments we all sat in silence. They shared their whispered unhappiness with the unavailability of low-cost housing. It was not easy for the people who gave Big Sur its character to live there. The illegal cabins they set on the edges of national parkland were being discovered and red-tagged, and kids like these, willing to haul water and do without electricity, were being driven away. I got the idea that Maria's place was a squat and her existence there precarious.

I waited until she sat on the edge to cool off, and then I lifted myself up to the edge too, opposite her. The time would probably not get any better, so I asked her, in a whisper, which for me wasn't easy: "Excuse me, this may sound a little funny, but around two years ago, did you meet a man here, a man who came on a Harley? A man around sixty, sixty-two?"

She and the boys looked at me with bemused expressions.

"Wow," she said softly. The boys just kind of tilted their heads. One of them giggled. It occurred to me they might have been high. It seemed a good time and place for getting high.

"Sounds like Adam," said one of the boys.

"Sounds like," she murmured

"Adam?" said I.

"He had a Harley," said the same boy.

"Oh, the Harley," she sighed.

I was excited. Adam seemed a likely alias. Same first initial, new man.

"Whatever happened to Adam?" I said, as calmly as I could, like just another local who hadn't seen him for a while.

"He's around," said another boy, his head back, his eyes closed.

Bingo!

Maria said, "He makes his appearances every so often."

She was definitely high. So were the boys.

"Where does he make these appearances?" I asked.

"Out of the blue," she sighed.

"Do you know where he lives?"

"Down the street, around the corner, and inside his own head," she said, and the boys giggled.

"When you see him, do this," I said, reaching across and touching my finger to her forehead, startling her. She did seem to wake up. "That's what they do around here to evict you from your head."

Muted and in slo-mo, they thought I was a riot,.

"How do you know Adam?" she asked.

"I'm his sister."

"Get out."

"You didn't know he had a sister, huh?"

"And you don't know where he lives?"

"No one does. He fell out of sight."

"True that. Listen, can you get him to move that bike out of my shed?"

Maybe it was the hot springs; I thought I was going to pass out. I took a few deep breaths.

"You have the Harley?"

"Parked in my shed, taking up, like, *all* the space. He really ought to sell it; it's worth something, and he can use the money."

"He can't part with it. It's his Dai-jô."

So I told them the story of the Dai-jô, as I remembered it from the cassette: the Great Raft, which the Zen Buddhists say you should release once you get to the other side of the river, but most people can't because they've cemented an attachment to what gets them through the day.

"Awesome!" was their consensus.

I gave them a few moments to mull it over.

Said Maria: "I never did release the raft. The raft dumped me in the middle of the river."

"Did your raft have a name?"

"You'd call him 'brother.'"

My head swirled with visions of the two of them.

"Don't take it inappropriately, but you're damn near breathtaking, and Adam, last time I saw him, was already out of breath. He dumped *you*? Somebody ought to talk to him, recommend a book."

They giggled some more, and Adonis One said, "What's the difference?"

She thought about it and looked at me, but I didn't understand the question, if there was one. "What?"

"He wants to know what the difference is."

"Who doesn't?" They all kept up the giggle of it. "All the difference in the world. If the motorcycle crashes, you didn't get where you were supposed to go. Wrong Dai-jô, wrong intention, wrong direction."

"Wrong, wrong, wrong," repeated the regressively awakened girl.

I was feeling pretty smug, like I'd killed a flock of birds with one stone.

"D'uh," said Adonis Two.

"I can't believe you're saying that, Dean."

"C'mon, be realistic."

"And I really can't believe you're saying 'be realistic,'" she added.

Dean apologized for being realistic.

I knew then that I was going to find Alex. It was now just a matter of time.

"In July, when the fires came," she said, "and we had to evacuate, I was crazy loading up the car, hysterical, trying to find my dog and take everything at once, and up walks Adam in his leathers. He goes, leave it all behind. So I put on my leather pants and my old leather jacket. He gave me a helmet and we got on that Harley and rode up to Santa Cruz. Stayed there for a week, laid around on the beach. Happiest week of my life. Didn't know if my house burned down, didn't care. Then we came back to find it still there, the dog was back, and everything was all right. That's the last time he rode the Harley. I don't know why."

"Dai-jô, bye-bye," said the cute kid named Dean.

"It's still there in my shed."

"And where is he living now?" I asked.

"You'd never find it," she said. "I'll have to take you there."

Twenty-four

I slept fitfully. I wasn't able to talk Maria into taking me to Alex that very night and I worried she would ditch me, or, more likely, forget she had ever talked to me. In the morning, right after a breakfast of steel-cut oatmeal and a soft-boiled egg, I exchanged email addresses with my new friend Bebe and checked out of Esalen. I followed the directions Maria had given me to her house. I was full of uncertainties. What if somehow Adam was not Alex? But it *had* to be Alex; everything indicated that. What if she had blown me off with bogus directions to her house? But why would she? Why *wouldn't* she? I had, after all, given a bogus email address to Bebe.

Several times I was sure I was lost in the wilderness, pushing my rented Ford over winding dirt roads, through moving morning fog, until, with great relief, I came upon her one-room cabin, with a small shed to one side and a cistern for water.

An Australian blue heeler tried to herd the car as I drove up to the front deck. Maria came through an open doorway and waved. I got out of the car and made friends with the dog. She offered me coffee, and though I was antsy to get going, I had a cup. The sun was already starting to burn through the fog, but we sat inside where she had a nice fire going and it was warmer. I saw some macrame, some pottery, some watercolor stuff, some bells, books, and candles, enough to make me believe that she was either living tchotchke to mouth or someone was paying her bills, my guess a phat father somewhere because this was too far out in the woods for a mistress with her attributes to be tucked away.

"What was Adam like as a boy?" she asked, as she made the coffee.

How the hell would I know? He drew circles in the dirt with crooked sticks. He had to be called home to dinner, where he played with his food. Under the covers, with a flashlight, he read Jack London and William Saroyan.

"He was a lot older than me," I said, "so by the time I could have noticed, he was already out of the house. I mean, to me, he was always a grown-up, but the kind, you know, that you could hang with."

I guessed that much was true, if he had had a little sister like me.

I drank coffee by the fire but Maria stayed busy in a corner that served as her kitchen, separated from the living room by a counter.

"Did you talk to . . . Adam, since last night; did you tell him I was here?"

"No cell phone service up here, and a land line is out of the question."

"Why?"

"He's off the grid. I mean, like all the grids."

"You still have some kind of relationship, don't you?"

"You'll have to ask him."

"What are you doing over there?"

"I'm making you a lunch, enough for two, just in case."

"In case of what?"

"Well, it's always good to have a bag of food, just in case."

It made no sense to me at the time.

We got into her pickup truck, the dog taking over the window, his head happily out in the foggy air, and we drove . . . and drove. I thought her place was a bit out of the way, but we went even more out there, until the road stopped being a road. She kicked it into four-wheel drive and we bounced over rutted and weedy trails, past the charred remains of last summer's fires.

I was feeling uneasy. I checked my cell phone.

"You're not going to get any bars out here," she said.

"Yeah, so you said. No electricity either?"

"Nope. Just a generator and propane. Kind of a different world for you, isn't it?"

"Yeah, but it's nice to know there is one," I said.

"I never did ask where you were from?"

I had a vague idea that Alex was born and raised somewhere in upstate New York, but I wasn't sure, should she want to talk about all that. I said, "I live in Seattle now."

We drove for what seemed an hour, but we were moving very slowly. Finally, we came to the end of the trail, just wide enough for a vehicle, where it looped around a small stand of trees and went nowhere but back. An old and battered Jeep Wrangler was parked under the Monterey pines.

She stopped the car and nodded toward an incongruous gate standing between two posts with nothing on either side but space. Behind it was a narrow path through new-growth brush.

"His place is at the end of that path," said Maria. "About half a mile, up the hill and down again. It's a yurt."

"Is that his Jeep?"

"Yes, but you can't drive to his house; there's only a path."

"Well, at least he's home."

"Probably not."

"His car is here; where else would he be?"

"He might be in the yurt, but if he isn't, go like this." She put her open palms around her ears, the way you do when you're straining to hear something. "Listen. Then just walk toward the sound."

"What sound?"

"You'll know it when you hear it."

"Aren't you coming along?" For one of the few times in my life, I didn't want to be alone.

"I wasn't invited."

"Neither was I."

"No, but he might be happy to see you."

In my own mind, I couldn't come up with a reason for why he would be. "Okay," I said. I wasn't going to turn back, not after having come this far. "This sound I'm supposed to hear? What if I don't?"

"Make yourself comfortable. He'll be back by dark."

I got out of the car and leaned back into the window.

"Back from where?"

She smiled. "You'll hear the sounds. You'll find him. It was nice meeting you, Adam's sister."

She pulled away, and as I watched the car bounce along the rutted road, I came to appreciate the danger of my position. I was in the middle of nowhere with a sack lunch and nothing else of any use. Good joke on me, maybe. I opened the gate, feeling a little silly, because it would have been just as easy to walk around it.

The path went up a rise. I wondered about mountain lions. I could always throw the lion my lunch and hope the cat wasn't too hungry. At the top of the rise, which was about the halfway point, I could see below the small round yurt. Behind and below me I could see a blanket of fog, but up there it was sunny. I walked toward the yurt.

As I neared it I called out, "Hello? Anybody home?"

I went to the door and knocked. "Alex, you in there?"

I tried the door. It was unlocked. I peered inside. One round room, and not that large. It did look kind of cozy, if not primitive. A camp stove, a wooden-framed futon sofa, some hand-hewn bookshelves, a padded chair, and oil lamps hanging from the ceiling. I pulled the door shut again and did what Maria said to do: I put down the sack lunch and cupped both hands around my ears. I heard birdsongs and the breeze blowing through the trees. And finally something else. A faint tapping. I closed my eyes and tried to isolate the tapping sounds: regular, rhythmic, then gone, then back again, off in the distance. I turned around, trying to determine what direction the sounds were coming from. I thought I had a fix on it so I started walking.

Never at home in nature, I missed my gun. I was anxious, which triggered a killer hot flash. I had to brace myself against a charred redwood and wait for it to pass, hoping I wouldn't start another devasting fire. I worried I might be giving off some pretty intense scents to any pumas in the pines. I longed to be back in the wilds of Pioneer Square and First Avenue, where, like Doctor Dolittle, I can talk to the animals.

Coming out of it, I cupped my hands to my ears again and listened. The tapping was louder. I resumed the hike. No trail to follow, I walked through ashes and new growth, stepped over fallen trees, and crawled up and over rock formations. The tapping grew louder. I pushed my way through some brush and was startled to hear a dog yipping. The tapping stopped. I came out of the woods and into a clearing, where a Chihuahua came dashing toward me, yipping away. I said something like, "Nice doggie, good boy," and the critter wagged its little tail and ran back to the man who had been sculpting a crouching figure out of a very large rock in the middle of a rock formation. He stood looking at me in complete astonishment, a chisel in one hand, a mallet in the other. He was thin, his blue-denim shirt wet with sweat. The shirt hung loose on him because it was bought for a bigger man. He had a trimmed salt-and-pepper beard and wore Ray Ban sunglasses. On his head was a broad-brimmed straw hat, long light-brown hair falling out from under it.

I thought, this must be Adam, but where's Alex?

Then I heard him say: "Quinn? Is it you?"

I walked up to the man I thought I would never see again, brushing some small leaves off my body. I held the sack toward him like a peace offering.

"I brought you some lunch."

Twenty-five

The sculpted figure, as much of it as could be observed emerging from the stone, was androgenous, crouching on knees and elbows, exhausted by the world around it.

"What are you going to do with this, once you're done?" I asked him.

"Nothing. What would anybody do with it?"

"Will you even know when you're done?"

"I have before."

"So this is what you've been up to for the past two years?"

"Don't you like it?"

"It's very impressive. Someone hiking up here is going to come upon it and go, Whoa!"

"That's the idea."

"How many have you done?"

"This is the fourth. They take some time. Always a figure of some sort. I don't know why; it just seems to work out that way. I chisel at a stone and eventually a person starts coming out of it."

"And then, what, six months later you sign it and walk away?"

"I never sign it."

"How do you find these rocks?"

"Just walking around."

"How far are we from your place?"

"A mile, two."

"Really? I could hear you working."

"Sound travels in this air."

"It was a hike."

"Do you want to have that lunch?"

"Yeah, I've worked up an appetite."

We found a flat surface on the rock formation and sat there. The sun was warm and directly above us. Maria had included a small tablecloth. He seemed pleased to see me but at the same time not happy I had found him.

"Do you write?" I asked.

"No," he answered. "I carve stone."

"There's no money in that, is there?"

"There doesn't have to be. I have a small patch, near my yurt, where I cultivate a few marijuana plants of exceptional quality."

"Only . . . everyone thinks you're dead."

"Not everyone, apparently."

"Well, I listened to the cassettes, the ones on your Harley. But even I wasn't sure. Shelley listened to them too, but it was just getting them that convinced her you were still alive."

"I don't understand that. I sent those to Gwendolyn way back then. Why is Shelley getting them now?"

"I don't get that either."

"And why does she even care?"

"She is your wife."

"Technically, she's my widow."

"Technically, she's not."

"She'll do better as my widow than she ever did as my wife."

"You know her house burned down? They're calling it the Tea Fire. *Your* house, I guess."

He seemed unaffected.

"You don't care?"

"It's only a house. I'm glad she's okay."

"Well, she's not hurt but she's pretty devastated, like on the verge of hysteria when I talked to her."

"What's gone is gone."

"Including all those cassettes and tapes."

"Good."

"Except for the ones she gave me, and the ones you gave me, which she really wants, by the way."

"Why?"

"That's what I'd like to know. I don't think it's purely sentimental."

"She thought it was a ridiculous compulsion, and she was right. A life doesn't have to be recorded."

"It's what your work came from, though, all those little things you saw and heard and felt."

"How did she find you?"

"Well, I guess you told her about me. She said you did."

"Yeah, I guess I did, but I'm surprised she'd remember."

"And I wrote a book about . . . all that, about Danny and everything that happened."

"You did? About me?"

"Don't worry, nobody's going to read it."

He smiled and said, "Maybe there's a movie in it."

"You can adapt it."

He kept smiling. "Under another name."

"That's how I wrote the book."

"How'd she know it was you?"

"Easy enough. Anyway, I just got a smile out of you."

"How did she look, . . . Shelley?" he asked.

"Pretty damned pretty," I said.

"I suppose you'll have to tell her you found me."

"That's the deal, but I'm not sure I have to tell her where. What is this stuff?"

"Hummus. It's good for you, Maria says."

"Oh. Are you sleeping with her?"

"Not anymore."

"Why not? She's young and beautiful and packs a good lunch."

"Everything changes."

The little Chihuahua was sitting expectantly, waiting for us to drop something.

"What's the dog's name?"

"Killer."

I gave Killer a corner of pita bread. He took it delicately and carried it away for closer inspection before chewing on it.

"What are you going to do about this, Quinn?"

"It depends."

"On what?"

"I think there's more involved here that just finding you for Shelley. I think there's a murder involved, with one more in the works."

"Murder?"

The carrot stick in his hand stopped before reaching his mouth.

"A few days ago a man was found dead on the Seattle waterfront, tortured and shot in the back of the head with a German Luger. A cop friend of mine called me down to look at the body because—guess what?— the only thing on the body was my phone number, my cell number. Which very few people have. The same day Shelley called me." He leaned back against the rock on both elbows, his chin almost on his chest, waiting to hear more. "The number was written on the inside of a matchbook cover from a joint called The Copper Gate."

"The Copper Gate? I used to go there. In Ballard?"

"That's the place. The number had a seven, written in the European style."

Now his head came up, looking at the sky.

"Did you find out who it was, the dead man?"

"A Romanian thief named Bodgan Michailescu."

The air went out of him.

"I was the one who gave him your number," he said.

Twenty-six

Killer came in for the rest of our lunch, and what he didn't want we left for the birds.

As Alex bagged his chisels and mallets, I asked him why he would give my cell number to a Romanian thief.

"I thought he was eventually going to need some under-the-radar help."

"What made you think that?"

"The story he told me."

"Which you're going to tell me?"

"He was a foreigner I met in a strange little bar. He had an interesting story, so we talked, but I was all messed up."

"Yeah. Still sorry about all that, but . . ."

"It wasn't your fault. Anyway, I gave him your number and said if he was in a jam and needed help he should call you. He asked the bartender for a book of matches and wrote down the number."

"He never called me."

"Maybe he didn't have a chance."

"He had two years. Maybe he was on top of it . . . or thought he was. What part of his story made you think he might be in a jam?"

Alex hoisted his rucksack to his back, whistled for the dog, and we began the hike back to his place.

"You saw my fish, at The Copper Gate?"

"A beauty."

"Nice to know it's still there. That's how we started talking, about the fish, two guys in a bar, but when he found out I was a screenwriter he told me he had a great story for me. His story."

"Like you never heard that before."

"Everybody thinks his own life would make a helluva movie."

"I know I do."

"Thanks for not trying to pitch it to me."

"Why should I? You're a sculptor."

"That's the nicest thing anyone ever said to me."

"You're going to make me cry."

"You're not being sarcastic," he said, in a tone of wonder.

"Sometimes it's hard to tell."

"Not when there's a tear in your eye."

I wiped it away. "He had a story for you. Go on."

"Well, he pitched his story to me and I must admit it was pretty good, if any of it was true. I'd just come off a terrific true story and none of that one turned out to be true, so I didn't take him all that seriously. At first."

"Why would Shelley want to listen to those conversations?"

"I doubt she would."

"And why would Bogdan be murdered behind them?"

"How do you know that had anything to do with it? He was a thief. Bad things happen to thieves. It's called Karma."

"Did you know he was a thief?"

"Yeah. He told me."

"And you gave him my number anyway?"

"You don't do business with thieves?"

I ignored that and said, "Where are those conversations now, because I sure didn't hear them?"

"I don't know. Look, he was a guy I met in a bar who thought he had a good idea for a movie, but I was already looking for a way out of that life."

"What was his story?"

We walked back pretty much the way I had come. There were no shortcuts. The little dog would run ahead of us, stop and wait, and then run ahead again, brave for a runt but not stupid.

"When the Romanian found out I was a screenwriter, he told me, kind of ruefully, that he had a story for me. When I showed a little interest, he perked up, thinking there would be some money in it for him. Wait a minute, I don't believe I actually started recording until he got to the gadangus of the piece. I wasn't sure it was worth it."

"The gadangus?"

"The MacGuffin."

"Wha? . . ."

"The motor of the story. The thing everyone wants. What he told me had potential. It was a caper story. Didn't have an ending. Maybe it does now." I was breathing hard from the hike. He was older than I and carrying chisels, yet he moved as though on an easy stroll in the park. "Who knows, it might have been good for a movie, but I was so distracted by the whole Danny thing I couldn't think of anything else. I was kind of out of it, kind of underwater. You all right?"

"I'm out of shape."

"I was going to say you looked good."

All women love compliments, and the fewer you get the more they mean, but where they come from means more than anything.

"Internally, I'm fat," I said, but his words gave me a renewed energy. I wanted him to go on with the story. He said we should save our breath for the walk and he would finish over tea.

It was a traditional Japanese *genmaicha*, he explained, a green tea infused with toasted brown rice. It was very good, soothing me inside, and revealing to me that the stuff in my cupboard was crap by comparison. His bed was a futon, which folded up to a sofa. We had our tea sitting on that, Killer taking a protective position between us. Alex stroked the dog as he told me the story.

"Bogdan was the youngest of a trio of Romanian thieves who operated all across western Europe. They were a little more sophisticated than your basic smash-and-grab gang but not by much. They didn't know the value of things but they knew where the valuable things were. They would hit a jewelry shop in Milan and peddle the loot in Nice later the same day, taking ten to twenty cents on the euro and in the end just managing to cover expenses.

Still, according to Bogdan, it was a lot better than working in a Romanian fertilizer plant. Like thieves everywhere they had dreams of someday hitting the big score. Bogdan told me that finally happened, by accident, in October of 2002. They weren't after anything in particular when they cased an auction house in Madrid. They put on their Sunday best and went to a preview. One of them . . . let me think for a minute . . . his name was Vladimir. Vladimir put his elbow through a glass display case and in twenty seconds the three of them scooped up some jewelry, some artifacts, and one other thing. The mother lode, according to Bogdan, though they might not have realized it at the time."

He sipped his tea.

"Did Bodgan leave you hanging on the edge like you're leaving me now?" I asked.

He smiled. "I believe he did. He wasn't a bad storyteller."

"It was the gandangus."

"It was."

"The MacGuffin."

"Yes, a golden bookmark."

"I'm feeling a little let down now. How much can a golden bookmark be worth?"

"Ah, not just any golden bookmark. This one had been given from one lover to another during a pivotal point in history."

"Okay. I'm gonna count to three."

He laughed. "You don't have to. It was given to Adolph Hitler by his mistress Eva Braun."

"Jesus! And they didn't know that?"

"Not until they had it. Vladimir was busted right out of the chute, but Bogdan and the other one got away with the golden bookmark. They finally realized they had something special. It was an eagle over a swastika over a rendering of the Führer's profile. All in gold. The two thieves could read German. The inscription was from Eva Braun. 'Mein Adolph, don't worry, it is only an inconvenience . . .' She had the marker made as a consolation gift after Hitler's army was defeated at Stalingrad. She comforted him that the final victory was assured and that her love was eternal, just as the Reich would be eternal."

"That's a lot to put on a bookmark."

"It was a large bookmark, six inches long. It was signed, 'Always yours, Eva,' and dated three-dash-two-dash-forty-three. What the thieves didn't know but would find out later, to their regret, is that among the bidders waiting for the bookmark to come up for auction was a neo-Nazi group, and they were pissed. They saw it as a crown jewel and believed the inscription was in code, hiding some fantastic secret."

"What?"

"I don't know. Neither did Bogdan. The neo-Nazis made a deal with the Madrid police to have a few minutes with their prisoner Vladimir, who caved like a fry cook's souffle. He gave them detailed profiles of his accomplices and Bodgan has been running scared ever since."

"Well, he's stopped now."

"Murdered for a bookmark."

"I don't think so."

"Really?"

"Did he actually possess the bookmark when you talked to him?"

"Yes, he showed it to me. It was a beautiful thing."

"How did he wind up with it?"

"After the thieves stole it, there was a major double-cross and his partner skipped with the marker. Somehow Bogdan got it back and made it to America. He landed in New York, then worked his way through the south and the west and when I met him he was in Seattle, still looking over his shoulder for neo-Nazis, his old partner in crime, and of course the police. All along the way, he was just narrowly escaping one or the other, getting by with petty robberies and menial jobs he could get off the books."

"Why didn't he unload the thing?"

"He wanted to. He said it was worth two hundred grand, maybe more, to the right fanatic. But to the neo-Nazis it was worth his life, so that's why he was afraid to sell it, even if he could find a buyer. It was life insurance."

"Okay, so why didn't he just cough it up to the neo-Nazis and cut his losses?"

"Maybe he did."

"If he had given them the bookmark, that would be the end of it, one way or the other, but on that very day Shelley calls me, hot to find you and your motorcycle and whatever cassettes are still out there. That's too great a coincidence. Shelley, or someone, must think you know where the bookmark is. Do you?"

"The last time I saw it, the *only* time I saw it, it was with Bogdan, and he carried it like a curse. Shelley would never get involved in something like this. She's rich. Two hundred grand doesn't mean that much to her."

"And your cassettes?"

"She ridiculed them."

"You know her better than I do, but I think she hired me to find you just so someone else could follow me, so that I would lead them to you."

"She wouldn't do that."

"We don't know what kind of threat she's under. She could be in real danger. So could you. So could I."

"It's been two years. All I did was listen to a stranger in a bar."

"Alex, back then, did you ever run into or hear about anybody named Bruno?"

"No, I don't know any Brunos."

"About a Stefano?"

"No."

"How about a German named Ulmann Maier?"

"No, never heard of him either. Why?"

We spent what was left of the afternoon trying to fit Bruno, Stefano, Ulmann Maier, and his leased van full of skinheads into the equation. I told him about Lars the bartender getting mugged by skinheads and a German in a fedora, about the same German buying an advance copy of my book, about the van that followed me to the Portland airport, about no-contract cell phones being passed from hand to hand. Part of that bunch had to be neo-Nazi murdering thugs, unrelenting in the pursuit of an artifact dear to the heart of their idol.

Alex made us a dinner of poblano peppers stuffed with black beans, rice, and cheese, grilled outside in the chilly night air over mesquite charcoal while the cook and his guest sipped margaritas. We ate the delicious stuffed charred peppers at his small table, by candlelight, pairing them with a bottle of 2004 Hanzell pinot noir. We listened to the wind whirling around the yurt.

The wine gone, working in concert, we managed to open up the futon and fall onto it and into each other's arms and he asked me what I was looking for, and I told him the ring, and he laughed and said that he threw it off a cliff at Esalen into the Pacific, and for a lovely hour all thoughts of Romanian thieves and German neo-Nazis and golden bookmarks and cryptic text messages and ex-wives and ex-husbands were out of our minds.

"I'm sorry I found you," I said.

"It's all right," he said.

"And I'm glad I found you."

"Don't think about it now."

I would fall asleep and then awaken, turn on my side and press my back into him, and he would put an arm around me. Once I woke up and was eyeball to eyeball with Killer the Chihuahua, who looked at me accusingly. I brushed him off the bed. Later, I woke again, thirsty from the tequilla and wine, and Alex handed me a bottle of water. We drank from the same bottle.

"In the movies," he said, "would this be a cute meet?"

"Re-meet. I used to work for you, remember?"

"And now you work for my wife."

"She told me how you met. That was kind of cute."

"You think so?"

"Sure. The audience would love it. A beautiful girl auditions for a role, but doesn't get the part. She gets the writer instead. Only they don't live happily ever after, because life is longer than movies."

He got up on one elbow.

"Shelley was never an actress."

"Then it's lucky she came away from the audition with you."

"No, I mean, she never worked in the business. I met her at a charity auction. She was with her first husband, an entertainment lawyer, who was crazy rich, and I was with my second wife, who was, well, just crazy. It wasn't a very cute meet."

"She told me she was an actress and met you at an audition."

"Yeah, well she used to construct different scenarios about how we met, to tell people who asked. To avoid feeling guilty about breaking up a couple of marriages. But those marriages were already well broken. I never heard the audition story before. She didn't even like actresses. Probably saw the ones I knew as a threat. And then she left me."

"She might say you left her."

I thought we were falling asleep again, until he said, "When a man leaves a woman, he believes he ought to punish himself. When a woman leaves a man, she believes she ought to reward herself."

"Why would Shelley feel threatened by anybody, beautiful as she is?"

"Beautiful women can feel threatened. Especially by women like you."

What did that mean? Okay, that I wasn't beautiful? I already knew that. But . . . that I didn't *have* to be? Was he saying something as wonderful as that? I found his face in the dark and kissed his mouth and we were awake for another hour.

I didn't check my watch but it had to be just after dawn when I felt him gently shaking my shoulder.

"Quinn . . . Quinn . . . wake up."

I woke up and saw that he had something on his mind. "Quinn, I've been lying here trying to remember. I never did record my talks with Bogdan. Nothing. On the night I was going to, I put the recorder on the bar but he stopped my hand before I could start it. He didn't want to be on tape."

"Are you sure?"

"I'm positive. I'd completely forgotten."

"So there would be no reason for anyone to be after a cassette . . . unless they *thought* you had recorded something either incriminating or revealing."

"Nothing. I recorded nothing."

"Before the Nazis killed Bogdan, they had him for a fair while. Those boys got heritage; they know how to inflict pain and not be bothered by it. A small-time thief isn't up for that kind of punishment. He would have told them everything. So why would they want a cassette, especially a blank one?"

"You don't even know who *they* are. You're saying Shelley wanted the cassette? You're saying Shelley is working for them?"

"Kind of. I guess I am."

"But why?"

"Look, whatever, you're safe here. Just go on doing what you've been doing. When I find something out I'll let you know. I'll get to the bottom of it, I promise you." The promise of a woman half-awake. I didn't want to get out of bed. I pulled the covers up to my chin and burrowed in again. "Now, let's get to the important stuff. On one of the cassettes you said you didn't like musical theatre. You wouldn't go to the *Cats* cast party."

"Yeah, I'd rather see a good movie."

"My kind of guy."

"I'll make some coffee," he said.

Lying there, I tried to picture Alex and Bogdan at The Copper Gate. Drinks on the bar. The recorder sitting on the bar between them. Lars behind the bar. Alex gives my number to the Romanian, who writes it down, puts the matchbook into his pocket. They talk about the story. Bogdan talks; Alex listens.

"Did you tell him anything about Danny?"

"I wasn't talking to anybody about that, not even you."

"No, you'd fired me by then. Did you tell him you were taking off, on the bike, to parts unknown?"

"No. Why would I?"

"Maybe just making small talk."

"There was nothing small about that. Look at me now."

I did. He was going to be big trouble for me, but some trouble you let yourself fall into. He turned back to the coffee.

"Did you even know, yourself, that night, that you were taking off?"

He stopped to think about it. "No. No, I really didn't. It was the next day, I think, that I got that call from Danny's mother . . ."

"Celeste."

"I can't bring myself to say her name. Two days after that, I took it on . . . What do you say?"

"The arfy-darfy. You took it on the arfy-darfy. And that was the last time you ever talked to or saw Bodgan?"

"Or Celeste or Danny or you."

I went back to the image in my mind. Two guys at a bar. Lars behind the bar.

"You asked Lars for a piece of wire."

"Who's Lars?"

"The young bartender."

"I never asked him for any wire."

"He said you did. Like, maybe for a bar bet or something."

"I don't do that kind of stuff, bar bets."

"Then maybe Bodgan did."

"I don't remember that. Seems unlikely. Is it important?"

"I don't know. That night, did you ever leave Bodgan alone, like, to go to the men's room or something?"

"I must have gone to the men's room. At least once. We were drinking. He must have, too. I can't really remember. Why do you ask?"

"Just pulling together the picture."

"Okay. Let's say I went to the bathroom. Bogdan's sitting at the bar."

"Got it. You with me?"

"No, I'm in the men's room."

"Well, come on out and stand at the end of the bar. What do you see?"

"My big fish. A worried Romanian. Some local talent."

"Focus, why don't you?"

"What do *you* see?"

"A piece of wire. And the recorder. You left the recorder on the bar."

He put down the coffee pot. "Okay, what's the wire for?"

"I don't know, but the recorder must have had a cassette in it."

He poured the coffee and carried the two mugs to the bed. I scooted up and he handed me a mug. He sat down next to me, his legs stretched out next to mine. I could feel him through the blanket.

"What was on that cassette?" I asked him.

"Nothing. I knew we'd be talking about his story, so I'm sure I loaded up with a fresh one."

"Okay. Two, three days later, you took off. What did you record on it during that time?"

I blew on my coffee, tilted my head toward him, catching his small sigh of remembering something he would rather not.

"That call from Celeste," he said finally, "the last call. Then I recorded my good-bye to you and gave the cassette to your Indian friends on my way out of town. I couldn't face you."

"I would have tried to stop you." He looked at me doubtfully. "I would have," I insisted.

"No, you wouldn't. You're a realist."

I couldn't deny it, as much as I wanted to, but in a moment I would prove I wasn't much of a realist.

"Why would anyone want that cassette?" he asked, reasonably.

Anybody but me? I might have said. I've had it with me, always, for over two years. Some realist.

"I've got it in my purse," I admitted.

"That cassette? Why?"

Busted.

"Figure it out. I must have loved you a little, then."

"Quinn . . ."

"Don't say anything. Please. Let's go back to that bar, The Copper Gate."

He sighed again, sorry for whatever he had cost me, and I didn't know yet the total tab.

"We're going to have to talk about this eventually," he said.

"Maybe not. We'll see. But back to the bar."

"Okay. Am I in the men's room?"

"Yes, at the time, but for now you can join me at the end of the bar and watch: Bogdan sits there, worried like you said. He's got Nazis after him. He's got his partner in crime after him. He's got Interpol after him. He was hoping to score some legitimate getaway money on his movie idea, but by now he gets it that that isn't going to happen. He's weighted down by that damn bookmark that he can't give up and he can't keep much longer. He's got to hide it, put it in a safe place. When you hide a treasure, you make a treasure map, so that you can find it again, or if you're not around someone you trust can find it. The map becomes as good as the gadangus itself. But then you've got to hide the map as well."

"So you are a movie fan."

"If there're sword fights."

He said, "Okay, so we're at the bar. I come back from the men's room and what do I see? Bogdan drawing a treasure map? Not the case. I see him just having his drink and . . . oh, God!"

"What?"

"I don't see him at all."

"Huh?"

He put down his mug and got off the bed, suddenly agitated. "Quinn . . . I'm sorry. Look, it was two years ago, more."

"He left the bar?"

"I went to the bathroom twice. The second time . . ."

"Spit it out, Alex. What do you remember?"

"I come out of the men's room. I look down the bar, but this time Bogdan isn't there. He's gone. Left me with the bill, which is okay. He's broke and I have money. I finish my aquavit, put the recorder in one of the pockets of my motorcycle jacket, hop on my bike and go back to the island on the ferry."

"You were on the motorcycle that night?"

"See? I'm a terrible witness."

"No, you're not. Nobody remembers everything at once. It comes back piecemeal most times. Little things you've forgotten come back to you." Then I dished a little attitude. I can't help myself: "Like being on a MOTORCYCLE. Like getting DITCHED and stuck with the TAB."

"Are we having our first spat?"

"No, we had that back then. But I got a question. This is a big question. Try to remember. The call from Celeste and your goodbye to me were both on that cassette. What was on the other side? The flip side. The B side. Side Two. What was on that?"

"D'uh? You've got it in your purse. You could just LISTEN to it."

Pitch a little attitude, you're going to catch a little attitude.

Twenty-seven

I went to my purse, forgetting I was naked, and unzipped the little inner pocket where I kept Krapp's last cassette.

"Where's your recorder?" I asked.

"What?"

He was taking me in. It hardly made sense, but I hurriedly threw my clothes on. "I look better in moonlight," I said.

"No complaints in the early morn'."

"The recorder?"

"I threw that away somewhere in Petaluma."

"You never got another?"

He shook his head. I had one, the one I was using on the trip, but it was back in my car and my car was at Maria's house.

"We have to go to Maria's house," I said, "right now."

"I doubt she's up. She likes to go to bed late."

"Well, gee, I hope that wasn't a problem for you." More of the attitude was leaking out, and so early in the day. He didn't take the bait, which you've got to admire. "We don't have to wake her up, I just have to get into my car and get my recorder."

"I really doubt there's anything on the other side of that cassette. I gave it to you right after I recorded my good-bye."

"The only way we'll know is for you to get your clothes on, crank up that old Jeep you've got at the trailhead, and take me to Maria's house."

And that's what we did, the runty dog in the backseat, its oversized ears flapping in the wind. Maria's mutt came barking toward the Jeep when we pulled up. Alex put Killer on the ground and the two dogs went off to play, another odd couple. I got out of the Jeep, trying to walk like nothing hurt after the bumpy ride. I went to my car and took the recorder out of the glove compartment and popped in the cassette, on the B side. I had to wind the tape to the beginning. I pressed PLAY and heard only the movement of the empty tape. I let the tape run on. Nothing.

"Half-hour each side, right?"

"Right."

We got into my car and sat side by side, waiting to hear if anything at all was on the tape.

Maria came out on her porch, a robe cinched around her. She stood there looking at us, a blank expression on her face. After another few minutes she turned and went back into the house.

"Would you like to talk about it now?" he asked.

"Sure," I said, but I really didn't.

"I knew you were attracted to me that first day we met in LA."

"I guess a person knows. Like, I knew you weren't attracted to me."

"That's not entirely true. I couldn't go there, for a number of reasons. My marriage was teetering on the brink, and if it crashed I wanted the end to be uncomplicated by infidelity. And you were working for me, in a position totally outside of my experience. I'd never even met a private detective before. And Danny in the center of it all."

"You're still calling it 'Danny.'"

"I mean the whole mess."

"Okay, not the best of circumstances for two . . . mature people to hook up, and that's not counting the hormonal firestorm I was trying to find my way out of. Sure, I was attracted to you, I had a few fantasies, but I could see you and I lived in two different worlds. I wasn't going to make a fool of myself."

"You were hoping I would make a fool of myself."

"Yeah, it's a man's job."

"We still live in two different worlds."

"I'm not all that committed to mine."

"You want to come live in an illegal yurt? With an old guy who goes out every morning and changes the shapes of random rocks?"

"Everybody should have a hobby. By the way, was that an invitation?"

"If you're smart you'll refuse it."

"No one's ever gone public to call me smart."

"You'd get bored and frustrated with me. I never go anywhere or do anything. You're a woman of action; I'm a man of . . . something else. I've never even fired a gun."

"I can teach you. It's not rocket science."

"You'll tell me things and I won't remember, maybe not even hear them."

"What things?"

"Things like, 'My father died today.'"

"I'm an orphan, so relax."

"I've had three wives and they all said I never listened to them. They all said I was lost in my own head."

"Three wives and at least one knock-out girlfriend of a younger generation."

"And some stuff you'll never let slide."

"Already forgot about it."

"You're quick-witted; I'm slow-witted."

"I had a lieutenant on the SPD used to call me half-witted."

"You're a Capricorn; I'm a Gemini."

"Let's call the whole thing off."

He took me in his arms and kissed me, laughter shaking between us. We tried to keep it boxed in, but it burst out and we laughed aloud over each other's shoulder. I jumped a little in my seat when at that moment I heard another voice in the car, a voice with a Romanian accent, speaking in a secretive whisper.

"My friend, this is Bogdan Michailescu. Forgive me my discourtesy."

I broke out of Alex's embrace and turned up the volume.

"I am afraid I must run again. It is all I do now, run. I know I can trust you. You are a good man. I have dropped the topic of our discussion into the gas tank of your motorcycle. Leave it there, please, until you hear from me again. If you never hear from me again, then do with it as pleases you. As you know, it is very valuable."

Nothing else followed.

"When I was in the men's room . . ." Alex started.

"Yeah. Bogdan went out and dropped the marker into your gas tank. Then, the second time, he flipped the cassette and hid his message on the other side, believing you would discover it eventually, though he took a big chance. You could have just recorded over it."

"He never called."

"How long did you have the phone?"

"Not long. I tossed it shortly after I tossed my recorder."

"So he might have tried."

"Maybe he did. Poor guy."

"Still, he had my number. He could have called me."

"Probably afraid to, wasn't sure he could trust you."

Trust comes quickly to some people. I'm not one of them. Alex didn't know I knew where his Harley was. I hated myself for testing him. "Well, we know where the bookmark is. Whatever happened to your motorcycle?" I held my breath.

He nodded toward a shed some fifty feet away. "It's parked in Maria's shed, over there." I let out the air. He had nothing to hide except his very existence.

We got out of the car and hurried to the shed. The bike was covered with a tarp, which Alex pulled off and dropped in a heap. He found an empty plastic jug and started to disconnect the fuel line.

"What are you doing?"

"Draining the gas tank. I'm going to have to dismantle it."

"Don't you have one of those magnet thingies? The thing that telescopes?"

"Yes, but magnets don't work on gold."

"I just figured out why Bogdan asked for that piece of wire."

He opened a drawer of a rolling tool chest and took out the magnet. He extended it and fished around in the gas tank.

"Yes!" he said.

"A bite?"

Alex pulled up the rod and at the end of it was Hitler's golden bookmark, wrapped in wire. He unwound the wire and wiped the bookmark clean with a rag. We both stood there looking at it. Light from the open door bounced off the gold.

"This is it," he said, "exactly as I remember it."

It was a beauty. My eyes went to the bottom of the inscription: Always Yours, Eva, 3-2-43.

A lover's gift to the monster she loved. I tried to imagine the occasion, and his reaction, and the path it might have taken over sixty-five years to wind up here in the woods of Big Sur, in the gas tank of a 1994 Harley-Davidson Road King.

"What are we going to do with it?" Alex asked.

"I'd say that's up to you."

He folded his hand around the bookmark and walked out of the shed, me right behind him, into the sun. We sat down on an old pine bench.

"Would it be wrong to throw it in the ocean?"

"Like you threw in the other thing?"

"Same ocean."

"I wouldn't lose any sleep over it. On the other hand, it *is* a piece of history."

He took my hand and put it on my open palm. "You'll do the right thing," he said.

It was stolen property, most surely stolen more that once, and the right thing would be to give it to the police in any jurisdiction, and I thought about doing just that. Eventually. But there were still too many questions I needed answers for and this bit of Nazi memorabilia might be the key to getting them. I put the marker into the pocket of my jeans.

I looked up at him. I didn't know how to say good-bye. He must have known that, and so he kissed me.

Maria was out again on the porch, watching us.

"Brother and sister my ass!" she called out, and went back inside.

"You might want to explain all this to her," I said.

"I'll try. When will I see you again?"

"I look at her and I wonder why you'd want me."

"Some things don't need explanations."

"The things that can't find any."

He kissed me again.

Twenty-eight

I would have liked to have stayed longer in the wilds of Big Sur, with Alex. Until I died would have been about the right length of time. Even though my job was over, or would be once I informed Shelley that her husband was still alive—and the two of them could figure out how to deal with that—I still had to know how she figured into the search for the missing bookmark and the murder of the hapless Romanian thief and the planned murder of someone named Stefano. She wasn't getting near Alex until I knew all that.

Heading north to civilization and more cell phone bars, and with Hitler's bookmark burning a hole in my pocket, I thought I felt a hot flash coming on. False alarm. It was only the warm echo of last night. I wanted to wrap things up and come back. I was feeling emotions I hadn't felt in twenty years. I even fumbled with the car radio until I found some Frank Sinatra. I just cruised, enjoying the drive.

In Monterey I thought about calling Shelley but decided against it. I was feeling too good. I kept that feeling all the way to the San Francisco Airport. While waiting for an Alaska Airline flight to Portland, I ate a pretty good Reuben sandwich at Max's Eatz. In typical overeater fashion I washed it down with a diet Coke. Then I found an unoccupied gate and sat down to talk to Shelley.

"It's Quinn."

"Quinn! Where have you been? I've been hoping to hear from you."

"The news is good."

"Tell me."

"He's alive."

There was a not-unexpected silence.

"You've seen him?"

"Oh, yeah, I've seen him. He looks fine and feels good." I wanted to say I made sure of that, but I kept it to myself. "He's lost some weight and grown a beard but he's fit and healthy."

"I'm overwhelmed. I'm stunned."

"Take a moment. I was a little overwhelmed myself."

She did take a moment.

"Where has he been all this time? Where is he now?""

"Ah, see, that's a small problem. He said he's not ready for you to know that yet."

"May I remind you that we have an agreement? You're working for me?"

She didn't sound all that sure. "Right. You hired me to find out if he was alive. Well, he is. You wanted to know what happened to him. Well, he didn't fly into the Pacific Ocean. He worked through a crisis in his life. He threw away his recorder and sent all his cassettes to his secretary, who sent them to you, although she says she sent them two years ago."

"Not to me. I just got them, as I told you."

"Whatever. You still want the ones I have?"

"Yes, I do."

"I'll give them to you. Anyway, he's decided he doesn't want to be a screenwriter anymore. He doesn't want anything of what he was before. So."

"I hired you to find my husband."

"Which I did."

"But I need proof. I need to see him with my own two eyes."

"Normally, I'd agree with you, but the man is entitled to his privacy. I mean, any cop would tell you the same thing, if you want to go to the police with this."

"I'm not going to the police."

"No, I didn't think so."

"The police say he's dead. They closed the case."

"Oh, they'd open it now. But nothing illegal has occurred, has it? You didn't cash in any insurance policies, did you?"

"No."

"So it's a case of a grown man deciding to drop out. It happens. It's legal."

"Why are you being this way? Oh, God, I know. You've fallen for him again."

"That would be unprofessional."

"You're trying to protect him."

"From what?"

"From me, apparently."

"Why would he need protection from you?"

"He wouldn't. Look, I think I deserve a chance to see him. Arrange it anyway you . . . and he . . . think reasonable and I'll be there. Anywhere."

"Maybe you and I should have another face to face. I'll come down to Santa Barbara and we can talk."

"I'm not in Santa Barbara right now. I'm back in Seattle. I had to come back."

"Great. Let's get together."

"But aren't you . . . ?"

"What?"

"Aren't you out of town?"

"As a matter of fact, I am, but I'll be back tomorrow. I'll give you a call."

"Wait! Don't hang up!"

"My phone's almost out of charge."

"It sounds like you're in an airport."

"I am."

"Which one?"

"Gotta go."

"What about his bike?"

"His bike?"

"The Harley. Does he still have it?"

Now, why would she care about that? Unless she knew what was inside it.

"I don't know," I lied.

"Well, he didn't sell it, did he? He wouldn't do that. He loved that bike. If he didn't crash, then . . ."

"The subject never came up. What do you care?"

"I know how much it meant to him."

"You can ask him when you see him."

"When will that be? Can we arrange a meeting now?"

"Shelley, are you telling me everything?"

"What do you mean?"

"Are you in trouble?"

Another silence, and again not unexpected.

"I might be," she said, in a completely different tone of voice. "So might Alex. That's why it's so important I see him."

"What kind of trouble?"

"I can't tell you that. Not until I can tell Alex. Call me."

She hung up on me.

Twenty-nine

The plane sank out of the sun and into dark clouds. We were assured by the pilot that when we came out of the clouds we would see Portland. I gripped the arm rests and shut my eyes, opening them only at the sound of the *thunk* that signaled a safe landing.

I crossed the sky bridge to short-term parking, eager to get on the road, but I was astonished to see that the white van was still there, parked across the lane from my car. What kind of persistence was that, if not German? Who gave such crazy orders and how long were they willing to camp out there? I could have been gone a week. I could have—and for a while this seemed a real possibility—not come back at all. When would they have given it up?

My cell phone had about one call left on it before I would have to recharge it in the car. I dialed 911 and when the lady asked for the nature of my emergency I told her the place and the floor and the number of the parking space and said, "There're three or four skinheads selling drugs out of a white van. They're high as kites, and I'm pretty sure I saw a gun."

I put down my bag and leaned against the wall. Inside of three minutes, airport security established a perimeter and two minutes later half-a-dozen Portland policemen joined them, guns drawn. Instructions were bull-horned. Windows were lowered. Open hands came out of the windows. One after the other, the skinheads came out of the van and dropped to their knees. As the plastic restraints were being applied, I casually went to my car. One of the goons, on the floor and waiting for the cops to search the van, turned his head and stared daggers at me. I gave him my sweetest smile, got into my car, and drove away. I knew I would have at least an hour's lead on them, and there was always the possibility that drugs or weapons would actually be found.

It rained all the way to Seattle, at times heavily, and I missed the California sun already. Along the way day had turned to night but only a seasoned Northwesterner could see the difference.

I got off the viaduct and stopped for the light on First Avenue. I turned south toward my apartment and heard the text signal on my recharged phone. At the next light I read it: "2moro, he toast." It was from Bruno. I turned right and dropped down to Western and pulled to the side. I texted him back: "How did u get my #?" I waited.

"You gave it 2 me."

"When?"

"When we made the deal. You backing out?"

"Maybe."

Okay, I never gave Bruno my number. I never made any kind of deal with him, especially to kill some guy named Stefano. This Bruno has been texting a wrong number. I wanted to turn it all over to Beckman and be out of it. Everything. Bruno, the neo-Nazis, Shelley, and the golden bookmark. And I should have, but the last time I talked to Beckman he failed to inspire any confidence. I still had that awful sense of something unfinished, and all the loose ends were still in my hands.

Bruno texted back: "Bad idea."

I couldn't leave it alone: "What were terms?"

"AFAIR Thanksgiving. Extend?"

It was like listening to Spanish. Sometimes you get the gist of it, sometimes you don't. "Maybe," I texted.

"Mo $?"

"Not an issue."

"Y or N."

This guy needed to be set up. But I couldn't sting him on my own, and I wasn't going to call Beckman until I had to.

"Talk 121?" I texted.

"We r."

"Real talk. Not text."

"Y?"

"Need 2."

"4Q/B4N."

Without a translator, I didn't know what else to say.

I sat for a moment, waiting to see if he would text again, but ten minutes passed and nothing came through, just the wind pelting my windows with rain. I wanted to go home and take a long hot bath with a short cold martini, but I worried that by now one of the skinheads might have used his call to tell the man in charge that I had given them the slip and was probably back in town. My apartment and office might be under surveillance.

I pulled the PT into Republic Parking on Western and reluctantly called Sargeant Beckman as I trudged my way through the rain up the cobblestone alley that leads to the Alibi Room. On my Rockports it felt like walking over tight little baby fists. Beckman wanted to know where I was.

"You know the alley, up from Western, that part from the hostel to the market?"

"You're going to the Alibi Room."

"Right. Have you ever been to the Czech Republic?"

"No."

"Me neither. Do you want to go someday?"

"It might be nice."

"I don't want to go, ever."

"Do you have a point?"

"This little alley always reminds me of Prague, especially on a rainy night."

"So in a previous life you must have been a Czechoslovakian who lived in an alley."

"Not necessarily, but there has to be some reason something reminds me of it and why I don't want to go."

"You never want to go anywhere."

"I've been told I'm a woman of action."

"Was this by an individual who wanted some action?"

"I'll slap you silly."

"You ever hear of Voltaire?"

"I know I have but when did you?"

"I'm a curious guy. Voltaire said, 'To be born twice is no more remarkable that to be born once.'"

"Jeez, you've been studying up."

"Okay, you want me to meet you in the Alibi Room. Why?"

"I've got some info on your murder case."

"I'll be there."

By that time I was already there, shaking off the water, finding a seat at a table and ordering a Sapphire-blue martini, straight up, olive.

It made sense to turn it all over to Beckman. It would be a relief. I ran a little debate in my head, but with the second hit of the silver bullet my train of thought was derailed.

They had a rack of free newspapers in the bar: *Seattle Weekly*, *The Stranger*, some other throwaways. I picked up *The Stranger* to pass the time as I waited for Beckman. I scanned some of the reviews: movie, restaurant, music. It was a gay paper and like the French the gays thought everything was shit. I turned the page to the theatre section and was rattled to see a picture of a woman who bore a strong resemblance, even in stage makeup, to Shelley Krapp, nee Lavendar. I dug into my purse, pulled out my mini-flashlight, and lit up the picture: a woman sitting on the edge of a bed with a man. Dawn Wyatt and Ed Barrows in *Come Back, Little Sheba* playing nightly at On the Boards. (*The Stranger* thought the play was an old chestnut long overdue for a decent burial and this might be the run that gets it done.) I went back into my purse for my magnifying glass. I held it over the face of Dawn Wyatt. No doubt about it. It was Shelley.

I leaned back and polished off the rest of my martini, rushing what I usually like to linger over. Impulsively, I took off. I retraced my steps back down the alley to my car. I was buzzed, I'll admit, but even if I were stopped before I could get to a motel I was sure I would blow below the legal limit.

The rain picked up again. I pulled the car out of the lot and onto Alaskan Way, heading south. When Beckman called, I was at about the same place Bogdan the Romanian was found dead.

"Hey, where are you?"

"I'm sorry as hell, Beckman. Something came up and I had to motor."

"What do you have on the murder?"

"Can I call you back?"

"You'd better. Are you coming back to the Alibi Room?"

"Not tonight, but I'll stay in touch."

I checked into a Sodo motel for the night, the kind of place where lost souls from Wenatchee take their cheap jugs and drink to forget. One of them, in fact, encountered me unlocking the door and wanted to be my friend. I told him I already had enough friends. Truth be told, not counting Beckman and my three Indians, which already is a stretch, my number of friends in this town still hovers around zero. I carried my overnight bag into the sad, musty room and tossed it on the sagging bed. I waited until eight o'clock, curtain time, and then put in a call to Shelley. "This is Shelley, please leave a message." Sure, it was. It had to be another of those no-contract phones, solely for my benefit. I looked at my watch. Right about now the woman I knew as Shelley, the one who wrote me a fat check, was on stage fretting about her lost little puppy, gone all this time.

A soak in the tub, in this place, was out of the question so I took a long, hot shower instead. I watched television, channel surfing to find something a tad more real than a reality show. I bounced back and forth between two different news channels, watching several takes on the tanking economy, respected experts in the field contradicting each other over the causes, consequences, and possible duration of the financial crisis.

My body no longer had the smell of Alex on it, nor the feel. I didn't really want to think about Alex until all of this was over. I won't lie, I wanted him. If I let myself, I'd think of nothing else.

Shortly after the final curtain, Shelley returned my call.

"Quinn, I was so glad to get your message. Are you back in Seattle?"

"Yeah, got here tonight."

"Are you home?"

"It's where I live."

"No, I mean, are you in your apartment or your office?"

How did she even know I lived in an apartment? I could have a nice little house on Beacon Hill somewhere. Kirkland, even. More importantly, why did she want to know where I was, physically, unless she wanted to tell someone else.

"On the move, actually."

"What's happening?"

"You and I have to talk."

"I know. Where shall we meet?"

"Where are you now?"

"I'm staying at the Four Seasons. We could meet there."

"Not tonight. I'll see you tomorrow at noon. Westlake Center, at the fountain."

"But that's outside."

"Yeah?"

"It'll be cold and wet."

"No, it's supposed to clear up tomorrow."

"Oh, sure, like they know."

She was from Seattle. I would bet on it.

"I'll have your cassettes."

"Fantastic."

"So are we on?"

"We're on, girl. Noon it is."

After I hung up I called the Four Seasons and asked for Shelley's room. They didn't have her registered.

Thirty

My ad-lib weather forecast turned out to be true. The next morning was the gray of a lambchop past its expiration date, but at least it wasn't raining and the wind was on hiatus. I bought three egg-salad sandwiches, a few Hershey bars, and a six-pack of Cokes at a deli. I left the car there, and took a bus up First Avenue to Pioneer Square. I couldn't be sure no one was watching my apartment or my office, but I thought if anyone was, he would not expect me by bus. I was glad the bus had to stop for a light on Yesler. Stop lights in Seattle are the longest in the country. Drivers have been known to fall asleep waiting for the green. So I had a lot of time to check out my Indians under the pergola. They were at peace with themselves and the world and I couldn't finger anyone looking suspicious or severely bald.

I jumped off at the Pioneer Square stop and cut diagonally toward their bench, coming up behind them. I laid the bag on David's lap.

"Tuna?"

"Egg salad."

"Yumeroo."

"How'd it go last night?" I inquired.

"How'd what go?"

"Were you warm and dry?"

"Toasty."

I sat next to Clifford, Hitler's golden bookmark tight in my hand.

"Didn't see you around for a few days, Quinn. We was getting a little worried."

"I took a road trip."

"Get out."

"Sometimes it's necessary. Went to sunny California."

"Glad you're back."

"I can see that. There's some chocolate for dessert."

When Clifford turned to check out the bag again, I slipped the bookmark into the breast pocket of his jacket. It was a tattered nylon windbreaker, insufficient for the cold, but like the other two he was well layered.

I hung with them for a moment, listening to a wrap-up of local street news. Then I told them I would be back later in the afternoon, Miller time, with a few forty-ouncers. This was, of course, joyous news and a bit surprising to the boys because I did not usually supply them with alcohol.

"What's the occasion?"

"I'll be alive."

Their heads turned to me, eyebrows raised, except for the one with a watch cap covering his eye brows. I stood up to take the walk or the bus to Westlake Center, and a skinhead appeared on either end of the bench, coming from behind us and boxing me in. I spun around when I saw the first one, only to see the other, who flicked his switchblade, business end my way.

David said in a kind of comical and exaggerated observation: "Oh, look, kids, they have blades."

That quickly, the one whose name I don't know stabbed his skinhead in the upper thigh, and Clifford Everybodytalksabout stabbed his right in the meatiest part of his ass. The skinheads shrieked like little girls at a Jonas Brothers concert. David Hidesbehindthesmoke, who on his feet towered over both the skinheads, cupped a bald head in each of his massive hands and clanged them together like a philharmonic percussionist. The bad boys hit the ground, their switchblades still in their hands, though much looser now. Their wails turned to semiconscious moans.

My Indians spun away from them, yelling, "Fight! Knife fight! Call the cops!" There was precious little fight, however, left in the hairless krauts.

David said, "Get out of here, Quinn."

I did, calling over my shoulder, "I'll be back this afternoon."

A crowd was gathering around the scene as I turned up Cherry Street and ran up to Second. I headed north, slowing to a walk, blending in.

Thirty-one

From inside City Kitchens I watched the urban waterfalls at Westlake Center, partially obscured by a tower of Le Creuset pots in which I appeared to be very interested. The clerk, unaware that I hadn't cooked a meal in two years and had no plans to start now, gave me my space.

Shelley arrived at the stroke of twelve, carrying a closed umbrella. I was able to track her all the way from Pike Street. No one was following her, but someone could be watching from any number of vantage points, just like me.

She checked her watch. She looked down the fountain on one side, and then took a few backward steps, and looked down the other side. Then at her watch again. She was startled, maybe a little frightened, when Bernard approached her. Curse of the brother on an urban street. He spoke to her, she nodded, and he gave her the bag of cassettes I had asked him to deliver at precisely this moment. Then he walked away.

I watched her look inside the bag. Again, she looked around for me. I took out my phone and called her.

"Quinn, where are you?" She sounded, and looked, agitated. "I'm here waiting. A black guy just gave me those cassettes. What's going on?"

"Are you alone?"

"Of course I'm alone. Who would I be with?"

"Meet me at Dilettante's. You know where that is?"

"Inside the . . . No, I don't think I know that place."

Right.

"It's in the shopping center, across Pine Street to your right."

"When?"

"Now."

I watched her to see if she would call someone. She didn't. She hurried toward the new meeting spot. I left City Kitchens and followed her from the other side of the street. I crossed over to Macy's as she went inside the mall. I waited on the corner to see if anyone would follow her. When no one did, I went around the block and into the Fifth Avenue entrance.

I stood for a moment in front of Fireworks, looking across the glass canyon to the Dilettante Mocha Café.

She was sitting alone at a table for two by the window, looking for but not seeing me. When she did finally see me approach, she gave me a little wave. I waved back. Once inside, I went to the bar and ordered a hot chocolate. While it was being built, I scanned the customers seated at tables: a marginally obese woman and a little girl who seemed destined to grow into her mother's body; a young geek on a laptop; two bearded, hatted, and tassled orthodox Jews discussing their open Talmuds; a good-looking young guy reading the *Post-Intelligencer*; two women shoppers on a chocolate break; and Shelley, her head still turned to the window. Was she waiting for someone else? She had the time to make a call after I lost sight of her. I got my drink and took it to her table.

"I got a number seventy-three dark, antioxident. How about you?"

"Viennese mocha."

"We'll feel much better now."

"Are these all of the remaining cassettes?" she asked, nodding to the bag on the floor.

"All but one. I'm keeping that one for sentimental reasons."

"Why?"

"It was Alex's good-bye to me."

"You don't strike me as a sentimental girl."

"Oh? How would you play me?"

"Play you?"

"If you got the part, you know, to play me. How would you approach it?"

She gave me a good once-over.

"I'd look for the one thing you want and the one thing you fear. I'd get down your walk, which is a bit inelegant. Your dialect might require a coach. I'd start a new spiral notebook and ask myself so many questions about you. Then I would audition and not get the part because they would have something else in mind. How do I know that you actually found Alex? The police couldn't."

"It wasn't that hard. By the way, he told me you don't even like actresses."

"Why would I not like actresses?"

"Alex and I had a nice long talk. Among other things, he told me he met you at a charity auction, not at an audition. He said you felt threatened by beautiful actresses."

"How odd. It was he who had contempt for actresses, complaining that they never said his words the way he heard them in his head. He called them female impersonators. He was the one who forced me to give up my career."

I gave her a limp round of applause.

"What's that supposed to mean?"

"You really are a gifted actress. You had me convinced, and even now you can't bring yourself to take off the mask. How did you do it? No, forget that. *Why* did you do it?"

"I don't have an idea what you are talking about?"

"The good news, *Dawn*, is that you got a little ink, your picture in a throwaway gay paper. The bad news is that I saw it. Up until then I was giving you the benefit of the doubt. I thought you might be in danger, under some kind of pressure. *The Stranger*, by the way, panned your performance. But they didn't see this one. This one you nailed, right up until the third act."

"I *am* in danger, Quinn, and I'm under enormous pressure. If you only knew."

"I'm here, tell me."

"You may be in danger, too."

"Maybe, but you're not Shelley Lavendar and you don't know Alex Krapp from Ish Kabibble. Let's start with that." She let out a heavy sigh. "So really, all that remains is for you to tell me what you know and when you knew it, as the saying goes on the senate floor."

"You're right. I am an actress. But I don't know anything. I was paid ten thousand dollars and perks, with another five-grand bonus if I pulled it off. That's a pretty good gig up here for an actress my age."

"And what were you supposed to pull off?"

"I was to play the role of the wife of this missing screenwriter and I was to convince you to find him. I liked the role. It was a stretch."

"Why, do you suppose, you were hired to do this?"

"I don't know. Really. I never knew."

"I can give you one criticism of your performance. You were way too anxious to have these cassettes."

"Maybe, but you seemed much too possessive of them. I was told that one of them contained 'sensitive material.'"

"And the motorcycle? You were keen to know about that."

"That too. Either the man or the motorcycle, I was told. Other than that I don't have a clue. And I don't care. It was a job, a performance. I was told no one would get hurt."

"Well, that was a lie. Someone already got hurt, like killed."

She recoiled. I had to assume that any emotion she showed me was probably an act, but if it was an act, it was a good one. She did look genuinely frightened and remorseful.

"Look, all I did was an acting gig. I'm a quick study. I prepped by absorbing your book. What I knew of this screenwriter I got from your book, and I used the feeling I could see you had for him. The rest was improvisation. I'm a damn good actress, but that's all I am. I'm not a criminal."

"Neither of us knows that for sure. The D.A. will decide if you're an accessory to murder. It would mean heavy prison time, I'm afraid."

I took a moment to enjoy my hot chocolate. She took the same moment to murmur, "Oh, God . . ."

"What about that whole business of rushing back to Santa Barbara because your house was going to burn down?"

"They told me to say that, and then to say that it had burned down."

"Ah, they. Yes. Who are they?"

"Three people. Two men and a woman."

"Names?"

"The woman was Nancy. I talked mostly to the men. Henry and Jake."

"Henry and Jake."

"That's right."

"Any of these people have a German accent?"

"No."

"Ever hear anyone talk about Bruno or Stefano or Ulmann?"

There it was. I caught a twitch in her eye, a tell.

"No," she said.

"So. What are you going to do now?"

"What am I going to do? What are *you* going to do?"

"Depends."

"God, please. Do nothing, Quinn. I beg of you."

"Your check cleared, so there's that."

"Why shouldn't you get a bonus? I'm sure that's doable."

"Aren't you curious why Nancy and Henry and Jake have spent so much effort and money trying to find a screenwriter they don't even know?"

"But you know where the guy is. You can just tell me and go away and tomorrow I can bring another fat check to your office. How's that sound?"

"Well, there's a problem."

"What?"

"You're going to have to report back to Ulmann."

"Who?"

"The man with the German accent. See, you twitched again. You're a good actress, but some things you can't control. It's really in your best interests to level with me." I took another sip of my number seventy-three, feeling those miserable oxidants heading for the hills.

"All right. I wanted to keep his name out of it. He scares me."

"For good reason. What are you going to tell him?"

"Whatever you want me to."

"Then you might has well tell him the truth."

She nodded, then looked up at me. "What *is* the truth?"

"Tell him Alex is dead."

"You said he was alive."

"I didn't want to disappoint you."

"He is alive, isn't he?"

"No, he's dead."

"But what about his bike?"

"Are you still in character? A man is dead and all you can think about is his Harley."

"Please, Quinn, get me out of this. I understand you want to protect the man, but just tell me where his bike is. What difference would it make to you? Or to him? It's just a lousy motorcycle."

"Oh, maybe a very expensive difference. Your German maestro thinks that a valuable piece of property was hidden in that bike, and he's right. Right now that gadangus is in my possession and I'm willing to make a deal. Go tell Ulmann that and leave the bonuses to them that fail, like the big corporations do."

A surprising calm settled over the actress. Now she was the one leaning back and taking a moment to enjoy her hot chocolate.

The good-looking young man brought his newspaper and his chair to our table and sat down. He opened the folded paper to show me a German Luger. Double da frick.

"Ulmann Maier, I presume," I said, as calmly as I could, knowing he had already killed one person with that Luger.

"How do you know my name?" he asked in a German accent and with some consternation.

"I traced the license number of the white van your skinhead goons used to follow me. I can see you're a man of a certain flair and you probably think of yourself as a mastermind, but it's pretty stupid to rent a van under your own name."

"You are a resourceful woman."

"Am I?"

"I did send two rather ruthless associates to follow you. You outwitted them. Then I sent them to bring you to me today. I was losing confidence in our . . . female impersonator."

"Hey, show a little respect."

"And I have not heard back from these associates."

"Skinheads. You call them 'associates,' I call them skinhead neo-Nazi thugs. You want them? Check Harbor General Hospital."

His eyes narrowed. "You would not have been able to accomplish such a thing."

"Like you said, I'm resourceful."

I was talking tough, but the truth was, I was scared to death. I kept hoping the chocolate would kick in and keep me from taking a nose dive. All that and fighting a hot flash.

"Shelley, please take this bag of cassettes and find a trash can for them," he said.

"Nice," I said. "Everybody's staying in character."

"Um, on the matter of the bonus . . . ," she said.

"Yes, come back for that, by all means."

"The woman and the two men?" I said, before she left. "Nancy and Henry and Jake?"

The actress winked and said, "Improv, sweetie."

She did as she was told. She picked up the bag, bussed her cup, and left.

Ulmann took my purse from where it was hanging on my chair. Under the circumstances I didn't object. He took my Smith & Wesson Ladysmith and slipped it into his pocket. He found the cassette and took that as well. He carefully examined the rest of my purse.

"It's not there," I said.

"I can arrange for a body search but you won't like it."

"It's not on me."

"I am a patient man, but I won't wait much longer to take possession of what is not yours."

"It's not yours either."

"The golden bookmark belongs to history. I want only to be its steward and to unfold its secret."

"The gadangus has a secret? Jeez, call Steven Spielberg."

"May I remind you that your life means nothing to me?"

"Hey, it doesn't mean all that much to me either. You gonna shoot me in a public place?"

"Yes, if I have to, and walk away. Do you think a public place protects you?"

"It didn't do much for Bogdan the Romanian."

Ulmann's eyes were devoid of anything commonly thought of as human. I didn't doubt he would kill me and maybe a couple of other chocaholics before putting a bullet into Shelley, or Dawn as the case actually was. Why should anyone, including me, die for a stupid golden bookmark, even if it did once belong to Hitler? I have a can of Skoal used to belong to the Hillside Strangler. You want it? I should have trusted my first instinct and turned the bookmark over to Beckman.

"All right," I said. "I don't even want the damned thing. Take it and choke on it. I don't want anyone else hurt over it."

"This is a smart decision. Where is it?"

"On a bench in Pioneer Square. I can take you to it."

He rose and took his charcoal-gray overcoat from a peg on the wall. How did I miss that? The man who had Lars the bartender beat up wore a coat like that.

Thirty-two

The young, fashionable, and articulate German psycho walked with his left hand in his overcoat pocket. My arm was reluctantly looped through his. His other hand was inside his coat, holding the Luger, pointed at me. The actress walked on his other side. It's a hike of several blocks back to Pioneer Square, and outside it seemed colder than it was an hour before. I was hoping my Indians had avoided being busted over the knife fight and were back at their post. The police knew them and would probably believe they were just witnesses to two skinheads going at it. I wanted to make this transaction as quick and as simple as I could. Of course, if I could find a way to bolt without getting shot I was going to take it. Otherwise, my only concern, apart from the Indians maybe not being where they always were, was how I was going to save my hot-flashing self once this creep had Hitler's bookmark in his well-manicured hands.

"No one knew what was on that missing cassette except the Romanian," I said.

"Yes, but he shared that information with me," said Ulmann, not volunteering how Bogdan was convinced to do so. I didn't want to know. I saw the end result: a body lying face down on Alaskan Way.

"How do I know, once you have the marker, that you won't kill me too . . . and Elizabeth Taylor here?"

She looked across Ulmann's chest at me as though that possibility had never entered her mind. I wanted her to think about it now.

"Why would I?" he said.

For the fun of it, I might assume, but I said, "To cover up the first murder."

"I never murdered anyone. Not that I couldn't. I trust you won't force me to take that step. I mean, I have nothing against it. The occasion simply has not yet arisen."

"Then who murdered Bogdan?" He didn't answer. He walked, looking straight ahead, ramrod straight. You might start to describe it as marching, but then you should stop yourself. The Germans have been ridiculed quite enough. It's our turn now. "Did Bruno kill him? Is Bruno going to kill Stefano?" I asked him. "And what did Stefano do to deserve it?"

He turned his head and looked at me with his cold blue eyes and said, "Your questions are senseless."

"Okay, so what about Shelley's house, the real Shelley Lavendar's house, did it burn down in the Tea Fire?" I didn't care all that much, but I thought it wise to try to keep him talking, and maybe Alex would like to know, if I could live long enough to tell him.

"Yes," he said, "it did burn down, but it was not the wild fire. I set it on fire."

"You?"

"A fire was already raging nearby. It was a perfect opportunity."

"But why?"

"My men and I had just stolen all of the cassettes."

"I hope she wasn't in it."

"No, I understand she was in Paris. She goes there every two years, October and November, so that she can avoid the American-election frenzy. I rather admire her for that, though the decadence of Paris is a poor choice."

"How did you come to know all that."

"I speak very good English, as you can see. People tell me things."

We turned down Cherry Street and when we reached the square my heart sank. The Indians weren't on their bench.

I sighed and said, "This is a problem."

"Explain, please."

"Three drunken Indians, street people, usually live on this bench. They're friends of mine, sort of."

"Personally, I have no admiration for the native Americans. They gave up too easily."

"Yeah, well, I doubt they have much admiration for you Nazis either. No one does, except for, you know, others like you. Anyway, earlier this morning I slipped the marker into the pocket of one of them, without his knowing it."

I braced myself for something unpleasant, but Ulmann seemed the soul of patience. He took a deep breath.

"A priceless bit of history. You hide it in the pocket of a drunk, an Indian who lives on the street."

"It seemed like a good idea at the time."

"I think she's playing a scene," said the actress. "I can usually tell when someone is performing."

"You do realize," I said to her, "that if he kills me he's going to kill you, too."

"Ulmann," she said, "I need a little reasssurance here, a word or two of encouragement."

"Stop all this talk about killing," he said. "If someone has to die, someone will die."

"That's hardly it," said the actress.

"I'm telling the truth," I said.

"It is ironic. When the tale of the recovery of the golden bookmark is told, this will be seen as a poetic full circle." Ulmann almost sounded philosophical.

"Where's the irony?" I asked.

"Mein Fürher himself designed the swastika, the glorious symbol of the Third Reich, based on a sign used by many native American tribes."

"Yeah, I knew that. You like the irony? It's yours. Look, my guys probably scored some money off some tourists and are off resupplying. They'll be back. We just have to wait awhile."

"Out here? It's freezing," the actress complained.

"We will wait in your apartment," said the German, looking up at my windows. "Your apartment has a clear view of the bench."

"You have an apartment down here?" said the actress. "You didn't tell me that."

"I didn't tell him either."

From the front door, up the elevator to the eighth floor, and down the hall, we saw no one, which is not unusual—one of the reasons I like the place—but this time I was praying for a crowd.

I unlocked the door and led them into my living room. Shelley—might as well keep calling her Shelley—took off her coat and made herself at home. Ulmann made straight for the window. He kept his overcoat on. The hand holding the Luger came out, trained on me.

"Nice place," the actress said.

"Yeah, I was thinking of buying it."

"Good timing."

"You think?"

She found the remote and turned on the television, channeling down to a soap opera. "This is my favorite! *Days of Our Lives.* I've been watching it since I was seventeen."

One thing I knew now for sure: if I survived this I'd have to move.

"All of this for a golden bookmark, Ulmann? Really? A house burned down, a man dead, God knows how much money wasted. And you still don't have it."

"If you are telling the truth, however, I will have it soon. If you are not, you will soon be dead."

"Look, it's nothing but a souvenir. A grisly souvenir."

"You trivialize. It is a national trait in America, I have noticed."

"You tell me, what about a bookmark makes it so precious, apart from the fact that it belonged to a little man with a funny moustache who put the world through a living hell?"

"I would be careful, if I were you, how much I trivialize," he said in a voice that almost convinced me to shut up.

"Okay, the Führer. Your living God. But still, there's gotta be some memorabilia easier to get your hands on."

"It would be enough, just that it belonged to the Führer, that it was given to him by Eva Braun, that it has elusively travelled the world, but we believe it has a wonderful secret, a long missing part of the grand puzzle."

"Which would be what?"

He never took his eyes off that bench down below the pergola. I calculated the odds of making it to the door before he could get a shot off. Not good. Shelley blissfully watched her soap, chin in hands. We spoke above the sound of sappy dialog coming from the television.

"You see," he said, "the golden bookmark held the Führer's place in a volume of Karl May. He had the entire collection."

"Not familiar with Karl May."

"Hitler's favorite German author, from the time he was a schoolboy. Novels of adventures among the Indians in America's early West. He intensely adored these stories and reread them again and again. A few of the novels were with him in the bunker at the end." He lowered his head, apparently still moved by the inglorious defeat of his master. "When all the good-byes were said, he gave the book, with the marker still inside, as a parting gift to Wilhelm Keitel, who was his chief of the armed forces. Keitel took it with him when he escaped to South America. The book was among the very few possessions he was able to bring with him, a reminder of his devotion and of better days. When Keitel was tried at the infamous Nuremberg trials and was hanged, his family bartered the golden bookmark in payment over some contractual dispute back in South America, the details of which are lost but unimportant anyway. The shame is that it fell into the hands of a lawyer. This scoundrel gave it to his mistress, a Spanish girl spending a year abroad. She took it back with her to Spain, and eventually it ended up in a Madrid auction house. I was there proudly to represent my organization, only twenty-one years old, prepared to bid whatever it would take to retrieve the bookmark. I looked at it with my own two eyes, sitting there with no more security than the glass case it was inside. Our priceless golden bookmark. But a gang of Romanian thieves—scum!—stole it before it came up for auction. One of the thieves was arrested, but he did not have the marker. I was desperate with fear that the two remaining ignorant cockroaches would melt it down for the gold. My organization put out the word among the underworld. We discovered that, true to the maxim, there is no honor among thieves. The one thief stole it from the other and I have been searching for him ever since."

"And you found him in Seattle."

"Of all places. It is beastly here."

"We like it."

"You are welcome to it. Where are those Indians?"

"You beat it out of Bogdan that he'd hidden the golden bookmark in the gas tank of a screenwriter's motorcycle and left a message on one of Alex's hundreds, if not thousands, of cassettes, so you needed that cassette and you needed that motorcycle and you needed that screenwriter to find the other two, but the screenwriter goes missing."

"Yes. I thought he discovered that he had the bookmark and that is why he went missing."

"Don't flatter yourself. His heart was broken. That's what we do here often with a broken heart. We disappear."

"A race of mixed-up mongrels."

"And we like it that way. Go figure. So you start looking for Alex Krapp. You track down his estranged wife and find a houseful of cassettes. Most importantly, a saddlebagful of cassettes made *after* the marker was dropped into his gas tank. You help yourself to the cassettes and burn down the lady's house so no one will wonder why they're missing. Why not? There's a raging fire going on all around it. In the meantime, you have my phone number, which you leave on Bogdan's body, which is *all* you leave on Bogdan's body. A weird touch. You learn I have a book coming out about Alex Krapp. You buy an advance copy and audition a leading lady from among the hungry pool of local actresses. She creates a role with a lot of buzz, and next thing you know, I'm on the hook. Now you're watching me, hoping I'll lead you to the screenwriter, because—damn—I'm good."

"Now you flatter yourself."

"Yeah," I said ruefully. "So what's the secret? What's kept you, or guys like you, pursuing this for sixty-some years?"

He was going to answer. He even moved his eyes from the street to look at me. It was at that moment that my cell phone dinged me that a text message had come through. I jumped with the vibration and the sound, startling Ulmann as well, who leveled his Luger in two hands. Shelley was still glued to the TV screen.

"It's a text message," I said.

"I should have taken your phone. Give it to me now, please."

I took it out of my breast pocket and read the message before handing it to Ulmann.

The message: "R U watching? SOB getting away again!"

"What does it mean?" he asked.

"Beats me."

"Who is Bruno?"

"Now, see, I was sure you would know."

"SOB?"

"Son of a bitch. Apparently someone named Stefano."

It was at that precise moment that I heard someone else in the room talking about Stefano. On the television. Stefano and family problems, the meat of every soap opera.

"Shelley, who are they talking about?"

Her head swiveled back and forth between me and the TV. "Oh, Stephano. He's an evil old man. See, he's on the DiMera jet and they're heading for Argentina. EJ is his son, who used to be a secret, but now Stephano's accepted him as his son. EJ has dumped Samantha for Nicole, and guess what? Nicole is having his baby. The old bastard will come around."

"Has he ever been, like, killed?"

"Stefano? Oh, most everybody wants to kill him, including me. He's been dead a couple of times, but they bring him back. The evil son of a bitch is indestructible."

I had been on my feet, but now I dropped down on the ottoman. Somewhere two people, one of them named Bruno, who had a friend visiting from Germany, made a bet on when a soap-opera villain would bite it. Telephone numbers were exchanged, incorrectly, one digit off, and it all played out on my cell phone. I asked Ulmann, "Can I answer that text?"

"No, of course not."

"But I have to. This Bruno has been bugging me for days about killing Stefano. It's all about this stupid TV show!"

"It is not a stupid TV show," Shelley insisted. "A lot of big stars have come off this show. I'd kill to be on it."

"Enough talk about killing," barked Ulmann. "Come here; send your text so that I can see what you're saying."

I stood next to him and typed: "Off to Argentina." I handed the phone back to Ulmann and sat down. In a moment another text came through.

"What does it say?" I asked.

Ulmann read it to me: "The prick. U win."

I put my head into my left hand and squeezed it. I felt both relieved and a bit ridiculous.

"Do you need to reply?" asked Ulmann.

"No."

"Good, because your Indians have returned."

I rushed to the window and looked down at the street. "Oh, shit," I muttered.

"What now?"

"There's a problem."

Thirty-three

Shelley begged Ulmann to let her stay until her show was over. I expected him to drag her along, but he seemed not to care, one way or the other. He told her she could stay as long as she liked. In *my* apartment, thank you very much. Buy this condo? Not now.

Ulmann stood still as ice during the ride down in the elevator, his Luger back under his coat and pointed at me. He had waited until we were into the elevator before he asked, “What kind of problem?”

“This morning I slipped the marker into this Indian’s jacket pocket, Clifford Everybodytalksabout.”

“That is a name?”

“It’s how he is known.”

“Go on.”

“I didn’t want to ask them to hold it for me because, well, they’re honorable men but booze is the boss and I wouldn’t trust them with anything valuable.”

“So instead you hid a priceless bit of history on a drunkard hoping he would not find it on his own person.”

“More or less. It was only for a couple hours, middle of the day.”

“And now the problem is?”

“He’s wearing a different jacket.”

We ran against the light, diagonally, directly to the three Indians sprawled on the bench below the pergola.

“Hey, Quinn! Wuzzup? Who’s the dude?”

They were, all three of them, wasted. I pointed that out, to their amusement and Ulmann's chagrin and disgust. I was sure nothing stronger than cranberry juice ever passed those Aryan lips.

"And you smell," I added.

"Eau de Thunderbird," said David.

"Eau de hell wit it," piped in the one whose name I don't know, and the three of them cracked up. They might have scored something to smoke, too.

"Where'd you get the money?" I asked.

"Get to the point," urged the German in a forced whisper.

"I'm afraid that is the point," I said.

"Guy with a funny accent."

"Gave Clifford thirty bucks for his fucked-up jacket."

"And he gave me his for a trade-in," said Clifford, pushing out his chest to model his new duds, a herringbone wool, three quarters length. "Which is way warmer than what he got from me."

I was dumbfounded. "Who? Why?" and in just the time it took me to ask the questions, the answers came to me. "Someone was watching me. Someone saw me make the plant."

The German's chin fell to his chest. "Ask him, please, to show you the label on the jacket."

I was nonplussed by his nonchalance. He was crazy calm. "He speaks English; ask him yourself." The German turned his head without raising it and gave me a convincing look. "Clifford, stand up."

"Don't believe I can, Quinn."

So I put one knee on the bench and pulled up the neck of Clifford's new coat. I read the label, but Ulmann already knew.

"Made in Romania?" he asked.

"As a matter of fact."

He took a deep breath and let the air escape like bad *chi*. He opened his overcoat and tucked in the Luger behind him, in his belt.

"Whoa," said David. "Old-timey heat. This dude bothering you, Quinn?"

"I'll let you know."

"The quest continues," said the German. He started walking toward First Avenue. A bus was pulling to its stop. I thought he was going to get on it.

"Wait!" I called. "I'd like to have my gun back?"

"Sorry."

"How about my phone?"

He stopped, found it in a pocket, and tossed it to me, a fairly long pass which fortunately I caught.

"What should I tell your actress?"

"You might remind her that an actress's life is full of disappointments. This would be just one more."

"Who killed Bogdan Michilescu?" I asked him.

"Why, the same man who gave your Indian his garment. The other Romanian."

He took the last few steps to First Avenue. The bus had already gone. He raised his hand for a taxi. It occurred to me that the quest might mean more to him than the gadangus itself.

"Wait!" I called out and trotted toward him. "So what was the secret, the secret of the bookmarker?"

He lowered his hand and turned to me.

"Do you know what a Shen is?"

"A what?"

"Shen."

"No."

"It is said that on the back side of the Golden Bookmark the Führer, near the end, scratched in a Shen, which is an Egyptian symbol of eternity. It is represented by a loop of rope. The Shen is also a symbol of protection. It is a known fact that Field Marshal Keitel hid in Egypt before he made his escape to South America. It is our belief that with the golden bookmark, the Führer was directing Keitel to Egypt, where he himself was planning to rebuild his Reich in exile. But his loyalists were scattered all over the globe, many dead, many imprisioned. Instead, he returned to his first love, painting. Somewhere in Egypt, where he lived a long and simple life with Eva Braun, there is a cache of his paintings. Who knows what other secrets might be revealed by the golden marker?"

I was going to tell him that he was quite insane, but why state the obvious to a man incapable of seeing it. Instead I said, "Well, Ulmann, as my Polish grandmother used to say, '*Stada baba nie ma gatchie.*'"

He looked at me with a slightly twisted face. It never occurred to me that he might speak Polish. "'The old lady has no pants'? What does that mean?"

A taxi pulled to the curb and he got inside. I stood for a few moments and watched it move up First Avenue.

Then I went back up to my apartment. The TV was still on, but Miss Ingenue of 1967 had taken it on the arfy-darfy. She didn't show up for that night's performance of *Come Back, Little Sheba*, or for the rest of the run, a big break for the understudy.

I washed my face and ran my wet fingers through my hair. I called Beckman and told him the whole story, including more or less accurate descriptions of the players. Then I took a bus to Brasa's, just in time for Happy Hour. Suki shook me out a Sapphire-blue martini, and I gave some thought to what now. I thought about all the missing-person cases—some missing, some, like Alex, in hiding. At the bottom of my martini glass I saw the future, or at least enough of it. I was not going to go back to Big Sur and Alex. He was going to vanish to some other place with different rocks to sculpt anonymously and to be grateful for it. Maybe he already had. Anyway, he knew where I was. Let him come and claim me. To any woman who frets that her bereavement was squandered on a man who still lives, I say your sorrow was well spent.

Author's Note

Here comes the *mea culpa* for hijacking the recollections of a screenwriter who had every right to believe they would not find their way to publication in someone else's book. I beg his pardon, but I'm sure he knows that all writers, like pig-renderers, use everything.

—A.A.

Caravel Books, a mystery imprint of Pleasure Boat Studio

Deadly Negatives * Russell Hill * $16

The Dog Sox * Russell Hill * $16 * Nominated for an Edgar Award

Music of the Spheres * Michael Burke * $16

Swan Dive * Michael Burke * $15

The Lord God Bird * Russell Hill * $15 * Nominated for an Edgar Award

Island of the Naked Women * Inger Frimansson, trans. by Laura Wideburg * $18

The Shadow in the Water * Inger Frimansson, trans. by Laura Wideburg * $18 * Winner of Best Swedish Mystery 2005

Good Night, My Darling * Inger Frimansson, trans. by Laura Wideburg * $16 * Winner of Best Swedish Mystery 1998 * Winner of Best Translation Prize from ForeWord Magazine 2007

The Case of Emily V. * Keith Oatley * $18 * Commonwealth Writers Prize for Best First Novel

Homicide My Own * Anne Argula * $16 * Nominated for an Edgar Award

Orders: Pleasure Boat Studio books are available by order from your bookstore, from our website, or through the following:
SPD (Small Press Distribution) Tel. 800-869-7553, Fax 510-524-0852
Partners/West Tel. 425-227-8486, Fax 425-204-2448
Baker & Taylor Tel. 800-775-1100, Fax 800-775-7480
Ingram Tel. 615-793-5000, Fax 615-287-5429
Amazon.com or **Barnesandnoble.com**

Pleasure Boat Studio: A Literary Press
201 West 89th Street
New York, NY 10024
Tel. / Fax: 888-810-5308
www.pleasureboatstudio.com / pleasboat@nyc.rr.com